D0931409

THE BLAZE OF NOON

This is a story told in the first person by a blind man. His name is Louis Dunkel, and he is a *masseur*. The scene is Cornwall, where he is staying at the house of a patient, Mrs. Nance, whose niece, Sophie, falls in love with him. Their affair, momentarily broken by the strange intrusion of the far more seriously afflicted Amity Nance, is recounted in a prose of great delicacy and precision.

RAYNER HEPPENSTALL

THE BLAZE OF NOON

O dark, dark, dark, amid the blaze of noon,
Irrecoverably dark, total Eclipse
Without all hope of day!

SAMSON AGONISTES

DUFOUR

THIS EDITION FIRST PUBLISHED BY
BARRIE & ROCKLIFF, LONDON 1962
AND DUFOUR EDITIONS, CHESTER SPRINGS 1968

© RAYNER HEPPENSTALL 1962

Library of Congress Catalog Card Number 68-11311

PUBLISHED IN U.S.A.
BY DUFOUR EDITIONS, INC.,
CHESTER SPRINGS, PENNSYLVANIA 19425
PRINTED IN GREAT BRITAIN

AUTHOR'S NOTE

This novel, my first, was written during the summer of 1938, much of it in Newport (Mon.), about whose streets in the evening I would get my wife to lead me with my eyes shut. No doubt as a result of such concentration on the idea of blindness, my own eyesight, which had remained stable since I was eighteen, deteriorated. I finished the book in London, during the Munich crisis.

It came out in November the following year, nine or ten weeks after the outbreak of Hitler's war. About noon on the day of publication, my wife rang me up from a call-box in Baker Street. Had I, she said, seen what some awful little pimp had written in *The Evening Standard*? I hadn't. I went out and got a paper. The headline stretched right across the page.

"FRANKEST" NOVEL IS CHALLENGE TO THE CENSOR

AN AFFRONT TO DECENCY

Story of Poultry-Yard Morals

Since the late D. H. Lawrence's banned book, "Lady Chatterley's Lover," no novel has been published in this country so boldly challenging the censor by its frank dealing with sex matters as "The Blaze of Noon" by Mr. Rayner Heppenstall. . . .

And so on. The telephone rang again. It was my publisher. The book was sold out. Outside their offices off the Strand, a queue of old ladies and of gentlemen in riding boots were offering three or four guineas for a copy. I was exhorted to keep my end up. My telephone number would be withheld. This would go on all next week until it was stopped. If it was not stopped, they could begin to reprint. It would take a fortnight.

Other reviews appeared. These said they could not understand what *The Evening Standard* had been talking about. The book was serious and distinguished. So I had a *succès d'estime* as well as a *succès de scandale. The Blaze of Noon* has been in and out of print ever since, sometimes in boards and sometimes paperbacked.

I am fond of it, of course. At the time, I had every wish and reason to celebrate physical love. I thought of myself as a poet. A friend, himself a writer, had said that I could never write a novel. His mother had a blind *masseur* in attendance, and it was through the other senses of such a man that I tried to re-apprehend my world. Having once met the challenge, I did not intend to write any further novels. Not long afterwards, I was called up into the Army.

If there was a distinct literary influence on the book, it was that of a French writer, Henry de Montherlant, not (of course) the now-better-known later Montherlant of the plays, which I have never much cared for, but the author of the Pierre Costals sequence and of that hymn to non-sexual athleticism, *Le Paradis à l'Ombre des Epées*. I also had a theoretical notion that the cinema had taken over the story-telling functions of the exteriorised novel and that prose narrative would do well to become more lyrical, more inward. But *The Blaze of Noon* is a very simple book. It is not the work of a literary theorist.

The original edition contained a flattering and (to my mind) extremely perceptive foreword by Elizabeth Bowen, whom I had not met at that time (and was not to meet until four or five years later). It carried no dedication. I hope that Miss Bowen will now accept the dedication of this reprint.

R.H.

April 1962

Part One

He looked up, and said,
I see men as trees,
walking . . . .

CHAPTER ONE

THE HANDSHAKE AND a few words of conversation are enough. I rarely fail to receive the impression of a woman on meeting her. Usually I can tell not only her age, the general features of her character and so on, but also, more often than not, her colouring and indeed just how plain or handsome she is and the type of her beauty or plainness. For even those aspects of a woman which might be supposed perceptible to the eye alone have a curious way of translating themselves into another medium.

It is not so with men. For one thing, a man rarely uses scent, or if he does it is somebody else's choice and probably inept. Other people's attitudes to him are not so particularised. And everything about his physical presence is more conventional, less truly himself, more determined by social environment or the size of his income than by anything else. In addition to which the senses I retain are not so acutely interested in men.

This story of mine begins in a car driving away from the station at Gwavas and out beyond Pentreath and Trevillian to the house of Mrs. Nance of Rose Gwavas. And it begins with perplexity at my failure to make contact with Sophie Madron who was Mrs. Nance's niece.

The other two people in the car I felt I knew enough

3

about for the time being. Immediately in front of me at the wheel was John Madron, Mrs. Nance's nephew and Sophie's brother. He was a young man, fundamentally sound and likeable and fundamentally polite, notably so. On the station platform just now he had come up to me and asked with a certain doubt in his words whether I might be the Mr. Dunkel whom they had come to meet. Anybody else would have taken it for granted. Betty des Voeux, for instance, had wanted to sweep me up at once without any introduction at all. She was the third of those who had come to meet me. I gathered that she was John Madron's fiancée, more or less. She was sitting next to him in the front of the car now, half turned in my direction and talking quite a lot to all three of us, in a voice that would become more metallic still as she grew older. Betty des Voeux. A brassy, handsome girl, vital and self-assured. Her nails were cut short, and she was strong in the wrist. Her scent was one of those high-pitched, lavendery scents which only blonde women use and only those blonde women whose care of their person is superficial and amateur, half-hearted. A girl addicted to violent exercise, very attractive to diffident men, fertile, due to put on weight in later life and, I reckoned, anything but Cornish by extraction. I was not greatly interested.

But of the girl Sophie Madron, sitting beside me, I could create no definite image. And that was dangerous.

It may have been partly because she, unlike the other two, had not shaken hands when she greeted me. That was already a gap. I was left to imagine the sensation of her fingers, and I imagined them cool and, in contrast to the other girl's, sharp-nailed and well cared for, hiding

4

a palm that was naturally cool, but easily changing to become sultry and moist. I had to fill in the gap in some way. The first meeting is the only occasion on which people normally touch hands, and to be deprived of that piece of evidence in meeting somebody who struck me as unusual, interesting, powerful in some way, would always leave me a little panicky, knowing that this person had me at a disadvantage.

But there was more to it than this. The fact that Sophie Madron had not shaken my hand was significant in itself. I am self-conscious enough, and I know how remote from these people I must have seemed to them, standing there on Gwavas Station platform with my case beside me. I had been in the train for seven hours, and that for me was an experience of some importance. I like railway stations, full as they are of echoing cries and human excitement and the sense of wide radiation from a centre. Sometimes I feel that I would like to hang a tin can around my neck and sit in a railway station all my life. But to ride in a train for any length of time is anguish. The heavy, clanging rhythms hold me clamped as in a vice. And the dead vibration, now and then jolting and tearing at the stomach or droning on the eardrums in a tunnel, sustained yet not sustained enough to recede into the background and become negligible, makes a world which the desultory conversation of fellow passengers can hardly invade. I was dazed. Apart from the usual pathos which ordinary people discover in those who are blind I must have seemed a creature utterly distant, alien and withdrawn from the world of three young people who had come to meet me. And the woman who does not immediately seek to bridge distances like that between herself and a man, either by touch or by a torrent of solicitous words, is unusual.

Unusually plain, perhaps, and therefore diffident in the sense that a conviction of her own inferiority stifles her spontaneous impulses. But I did not think Sophie Madron was plain. There had been a trace of diffidence in her voice, but it was superficial and of a kind that goes rather with too much than with too little emotional readiness.

No, it was something quite different from this. Either she was a woman in love and obsessed and therefore devoid of any outgoing impulse towards other men (but I felt something a little too vague and tremulous about her for this to be altogether true). Or she might be a woman so fastidious, superficially, and at bottom so erotically self-conscious that she had considered beforehand how important and therefore how compromising to herself is the touch of a man whose eyes are in his fingers and had been shy and aloof for that reason. At any rate, she was passionate. So much her voice told me, vague and a little too deliberately languid. And she was small, to judge by the lightness of her movements, and very sensitive. And I was intrigued.

I was sorry to be intrigued. At that moment, I mean. It would have been pleasanter to have been allowed to accept the different moments as they came and live myself slowly into the newness of this little Cornish world until, as they say, I found my feet.

It was pleasant merely to be riding in a car after those seven hours of a cramped mind in the train. The movements of a car are sensitive and various, and the sense of human control is immediate. Holding itself hard around the corners and then pulling out into the straight of the road a car is alive. And the air was alive. It was unusual weather for April, hot and still. As we came out behind the buildings and on to the open sea-front the scent of a light breeze over Gwavas Bay had been exquisite to me. Now we were climbing inland, and the air was like silk, and high above us the gulls were crying.

But the sense of distance and spaciousness, which I find so difficult to achieve, was inhibited by my interest in the woman sitting beside me. I tried to gather more than can be gathered from the vague heaviness of her scent. It told me little more than that her colouring was almost certainly dark. I put my hand flat upon the rexine of the seat beside me and tried to gauge more exactly the stress and balance of her figure against the occasional lurching of the car. I could not try to make her talk, because I was uncertain of myself, being uncertain of her. And in any case the other girl, Betty des Voeux, was talking most of the time.

It was she, in fact, who provided me with my first piece of certainty. As we climbed the Trevillian hill behind Pentreath she had subsided for a moment, no doubt because the car in low gear made too much noise for her to speak through. Then just as we were coming up over the crest she turned round to us again.

'Sophie, darling. There's your proletarian. Didn't you see?'

The woman sitting beside me did not answer. I was aware of hard restraint and feminine weapons bared for

7

a moment between the two of them. Then Betty des Voeux had turned away and was chattering again to John Madron at the wheel.

I switched my mind back to its proper occupation of coping with the more general sensations of a new environment. And it was not so very long before the car was turning into a narrow, deeply rutted drive and then pulling up before a house. This was the house called Rose Gwavas, after the heath it stood on, where Mrs. Nance still lived when she wasn't up in London for treatment. It was evidently built in a hollow.

Mrs. Nance did not come down until dinner was served. She had been painting. She painted flowers and still had a ready sale in America. Everbody in England knew how bad her flowers were, she said, except the seed growers who reproduced her in their catalogues.

The two hours before supper had been mainly occupied for me in walking up and down the house with John Madron, whose diplomacy seemed to be taken for granted by everyone else as one of the household amenities. I had formed a fairly definite idea of the house's lay-out, sufficient, at any rate, to let me blunder around quite safely by myself from now on. The gardens, for the time being, we had left alone. Sophie was walking about the gardens outside by herself. Every now and then, as John and I passed an open window or a door in our perambulations, her footsteps crunching the gravel or her voice talking to a kitten had reached us, and once she had seemed to be humming a popular blues to herself in a voice that had very little tune and plenty of subtle

8

rhythm. Betty des Voeux had long since taken a cup of tea with us and gone home.

Sherry had been brought in by a girl who was, I gathered, the only resident servant, for even the cook lived in her own cottage about a mile away. A good sherry, but not unusual. John Madron had found plenty to say about the country-side and the house and had scrupulously avoided either asking me questions or telling me anything that I wanted to know. Sophie had come in, tasted her sherry, decided to have a bath instead, and gone upstairs. The girl had returned and pottered about in the hall where we were sitting, making a fire in what John told me was an open ingle of no architectural interest whatever.

Mrs. Nance came in.

'Good evening, Louis,' she said. 'Do you like the house?'

'There seems to be a lot of plain, white-washed stone, and you have thick carpets in the right places and wooden catches to the doors.'

'And that's nice, isn't it? It's called Rose Gwavas from the heath. Did anybody tell you? Rose is the Cornish word for a heath. This one has a blood lust. There was a sacrificial theatre in the garden. It's a great outcropping of granite, piled up to the height of the bedroom windows. There used to be a boulder laid right across one of the window-sills, but that's where the girl sleeps.'

'And I'm liable to be murdered by a Saracen man.'

'Yes, I'm so glad John told you. Where's Sophie? John, dear, go and tell Sophie we're waiting. No, tell her we're going to start now. . . . .'

9

Then a specimen of her social line:

'. . . Louis Dunkel, I shall have to take your arm, I'm afraid.'

She gave John Madron her stick, leaned her weight on my arm and left it to me to guide her to her place in the dining-room. It was the sort of heavy compliment she had paid me before, and I liked it. I believe she closed her eyes, too, as I led her in.

One of Mrs. Nance's fancies was to drink port after dinner with her male guests. Her port was better than her sherry, not, I imagine, because her taste in port was finer, but because the sherry was served to her women-folk, too, and therefore ought to be a little inferior. Her father, Admiral Madron, had been a port drunkard, and following in her father's footsteps had become the pattern of Mrs. Nance's life even, I have sometimes thought, to the point of developing the paralysis in her legs as the nearest approach she could contrive to Admiral Madron's gout.

I have always been surprised that the meek, stuttering little man, Mrs. Nance's husband, should eventually have run away from her. She so obviously possessed just those things he lacked. I suppose some ridiculous desire to assert his male independence had triumphed at length over all the rightness, all the mutual compensation, of their life together. He was, after all, an architect of some eminence and used, I believe, to stutter a great deal less with his male associates towards the end of his relationship with Mrs. Nance.

At any rate he had gone. Nobody knew for certain

10

where, though rumours had been heard of him as in Australia and then the West Indies, and Mrs. Nance had prophesied bitterly, just after his departure, that he would eventually find rest upon the bosom of some enormous buck nigger or negress.

'It wouldn't matter which so long as he or she was buck enough.'

And she had been left with Admiral Madron's house on Rose Gwavas and a nephew and niece just home from America, where their father had gone after the divorce of his wife and where they had spent the fag-end of their schooldays and three years and one year respectively at different universities. In the Rose Gwavas house and in the nephew and niece his grandchildren she had gathered together all that remained, with herself, of Admiral Madron, and she had taken to herself, one by one, all the habits and superficial characteristics that she remembered in him. I have been told that she had even grown to look like Admiral Madron, though she retained her page-boy hair and the long, hand-woven garments of her æsthetic youth.

Nor was all this the effect of mellowing age, for she was still, I imagine, only a little over fifty, and the trouble with her legs was in no sense the disease of a general deterioration. It was, no doubt, neurotic, but Mrs. Nance herself probably knew it at times and certainly did not use her disability to impose herself on the attentions of other people.

This was my first visit to her in Cornwall and my first meeting with any of her relatives and dependents except for one brief encounter with her husband, whom she had brought along to the first consultation she ever had with me, shortly before his disappearance. Now, on this first evening at Rose Gwavas, she had me up to drink port with her in the library and to talk for half an hour about her young people, as she called them, and it was a little odd to be brought to realise that the woman Sophie Madron, who had at once become for me an acute body of sensation or rather of the lack of it, on the station platform and in an open car, was indeed the niece, Admiral Madron's grandchild, of whom I had heard so much previously. It is, I suppose, rather more difficult for me than for an ordinarily equipped man to integrate scattered groups of sensations into a single whole.

Mrs. Nance herself brought the conversation round that way.

'John,' she said, 'is polite, as you'll have noticed. It's a vocation with him. Being polite is the way John has of making himself feel a complete man when he's still economically dependent on me. He's a lovely thing, but in any case of crisis he'll behave like an English gentleman, and that's where he fails as a person. Sophie, now . . .'

She cracked a walnut between her teeth and spat out bits of the shell, I suppose into the palm of her hand.

Her voice was a heavy one that lifted itself readily up behind her nose. She would have made a great singer on the Edwardian halls.

'. . . No, you can tell me about her, Louis Dunkel.'

'Sophie?'

'Yes.'

'I don't know anything about her.'

12

'That's what I thought. I've always been convinced she was a vague little piece. Well, now, can I tell you anything, Louis?'

'Please.'

'Colouring, for instance?'

'Please, yes.'

'Well, she's one of those Cornish girls with a lot of Jew or Spaniard or something in her. You know, a lot of black hair like the rest of us, but none of that lovely navy blue about her eyes. They're big, and they're brown. It's a fact, Louis, when they came back from America I thought she was a two-per-cent Creole girl John had picked up. Sophie could be American, I reckon. She's got that figure, mathematically precise, and those high cheeks and that way of wearing her clothes and the smallness of bone that you only find in hybrids. She's got the American boredom, too, I think.'

'And under the surface. . . .?'

'I can't tell you anything about that, Louis. I don't think anybody can. Nobody's made enough demands on her yet to get anything coming out through the boredom. Sophie's untried.

'That means . . .?'

'No, it doesn't, Louis Dunkel. She lays herself open. At the moment she's trying herself out on a young quarryman. I thought at first it showed the extremely sophisticated little sensationist, but it doesn't. He's not one of those buck proletarians the weary, middle-aged women go in for a lot down at Four Tides. He's a blue-eyed boy, and I think it's sentimental mostly, though no doubt the other thing comes into it. It's a sort of fancy, hard-boiled Communism, I suppose.'

'Has he got a name?'

'Nicky, I think. Nicky Polgigga. That wouldn't tell you anything, would it?'

'No,'

'Well, don't ask, then. I suppose you're in favour of proletarian lovers, aren't you, Louis?'

'Not just like that. I'm not prepared to legislate.'

'I see. I think I am in favour. It riles John and his friends more than I can tell you. John's a hell of a gent, Louis. And as for that—er. . . .'

'Brassy tart?'

'. . . Yes, that brassy little Major's brat Betty des Voeux. . . .'

Mrs. Nance had her very well marked out:

'. . . One of those P.T.'s of the emancipation, I call them. You know what I mean, Louis. It's still the old game of exciting the male without intent to gratify. The aim is still to tease him into marriage when necessary. Only since the depression they've had to play the game according to the rules of post-war morality. You see. . . .'

Well, I did not see, and that is why Mrs. Nance was exerting herself to people this new stage for me. I do not think she had a particularly analytical mind. Her talent was practical and intuitive, for all her maleness. And it has given me pleasure to think of her wondering beforehand how best to show me what otherwise it would take me a long time to work out for myself and putting her scattered impressions into some kind of analytical order to that end and on my behalf. I heard her get up from her chair and move heavily with her stick to a far

14

corner of the library. There she stood for a moment and then came back and got down to it.

It was the picture of a local gentry all impoverished. And that meant for the young people both that they couldn't marry early, and that in any case they hadn't any visible responsibilities about which they could be expected to behave in a responsible manner. And so the erotic code of less privileged classes was adopted, but indulged in with an awful self-consciousness and largely with the desire of spiting their parents who'd left them with only a small amount of money for their pleasures, not sufficient for a whore, but only for a girl of their own class who hadn't a car of her own. And at the same time they were greater prigs and more up on their privileges than ever their fathers had been. They did, in fact, feel themselves to be in some way superior to a workman. Sophie Madron's attempt to break out of the vicious circle did, in fact, seem to them to be something awful. And it was, in fact, because her Nicky earned more at the quarries, little as it was, than Master John himself had, apart from the car, which Mrs. Nance had bought him. The quarryman had a stake of some kind in society. John Madron was outside it. He was the true social outcast, not your exploited working lad.

'. . . . And that's where revolution is coming from in this country, Louis, not from the working classes but from dispossessed, class-conscious rich boys. They'll never be content until they've got their own back on the working classes, smashed their organisations and bled them down to what they were a hundred years ago. All this, you know, because their real enemies, the people who've got the money they need, went to the same schools as themselves and speak with the same accent. John's got that taint, and he's a lovely thing, I tell you. He'd lose it if he got among intelligent people of his own generation. You might be able to help him there. . . .'

I did not think it likely. In the meantime I was to take it for granted that he knew very little outside the game played by his kind all over the English country-side, not only down here, and the sense they all shared of being superior people cheated of their dues. Sophie was highly receptive and had learnt something in America. John had remained too consciously English. And any glimpses of rebellious intelligence were immediately inhibited.

'. . . Inhibited by a brassy, upper-class tart called Betty des Voeux. Her father's a major who's had to go in for growing tomatoes, and he hasn't a penny. She can't work. Damn it, she's been presented at Court. They still have connections. And so she keeps up this new, mixed game of Bohemian morals and landed-gentry manners. And just now she's keeping it up with my John, alas. They're engaged, I believe. Yes, they're engaged, Louis. And she sleeps with John when she feels like it. And that kind of hand-fasting is mighty fine among agricultural labourers who take other people seriously. But it's mighty un- pleasant among the local young gentry. For, you see, it's as much a question of values in the marriage market with Betty des Voeux as ever it was with the pure, wilt- ing girls of the generation before mine. If a better match came along she'd leave John in two seconds, and John would feel in honour bound to make no fuss. In the meantime she's not going to risk devaluation even in his eyes. She sleeps with John now and again. Always with reservations and always at wide enough intervals to keep his appetite whetted. To enter into any sort of complete relationship with him is the last thing in the world she wants. It might satisfy him. He might find her out. Above all things he must be kept in a state of fundamental dissatisfaction so that at any moment, if she gave up hope of a better match, she could deny him for a longer period than usual until he came begging at her, ready for marriage or anything she liked. The P.T.'s of the emancipation, Louis. That's what I call them.'

She took a deep breath and had me fill up her glass and my own. And that was that.

I contributed nothing. Mrs. Nance did not expect me to. I am not myself implicated in these questions. The excessively rich are my employers, and I myself am classless, though I have affinities with the intolerably poor. I had to have the stage peopled for me, and this would do for the time being. I drank enough of Mrs. Nance's fine port to take all the edges off things and was presently dismissed. Mrs. Nance ordered me to bed for a good, long rest as a preparation for beating her up in the morning, but, in fact, gave me a careful description of the general lay-out of the gardens near the house in case I felt like disobeying her.

'There isn't a moon up,' she said.

And I remember that she was pouring more of the good port into her glass as I found my way out of the library. I went downstairs and stood for a moment in the hall. Nobody was there. I heard nothing but the rustle of burning wood in the open fireplace and then the

17

sound of a car, some distance from the house, which might have been John Madron turning out of the drive or merely somebody passing along the road. The smell of the wood smoke gave me an exquisite nostalgia. I recalled lanes in Essex and in Kent where I had walked at night and retained my sense of human indwelling only from the smells of wood smoke which had reached me, as I came towards a farm or an isolated cottage, always two or three seconds before the dogs ever got my scent and broke into their muffled barking, whining and dragging at their chains.

I went out and had the gravel crunching beneath my feet until I touched the first of the granite that came up here to within two or three yards of one side of the house. The fracture of the granite was horizontal, making it reveal itself, beneath the erosions of wind and rain, as a series of enormous flat slabs, almost like the wafers of a great bed of slate, piled up one on top of another to a considerable height. I climbed up perhaps twenty feet and at the point I eventually came to tapped around me with one foot until I knew that I was on a more or less even surface extending for possibly thirty yards in a single direction before there was any break at all. I reckoned that beyond the fissures which bordered this single great slab the granite must have covered a good many acres of ground and completely shut in one side of the house and a long stretch of the drive. It was impressive. John had already told me some of the legends, and I knew that local tradespeople, not the most imaginative of men, although these were Cornish and therefore no doubt superstitious, were often very reluctant to deliver their goods here, although Mrs. Nance's was the most reliable money for miles around. I stood perfectly still and breathed in the night scents of the garden. I must have trembled a little with a profound weakness. I was afflicted with the nostalgia of sight which I had spent then some fifteen years in the attempt to eradicate. It would pass. It was the effect of all this newness around me and the greater slowness of adjustment which is the one fundamental disability those like me are impeded with. I felt a need for colour and light. In the place where I stood there should have been strange effects of moonlight drawing out concealed subtleties of colour in the grain of the granite. I knelt down for a while to feel the surface of the granite with my fingers, the dull bosses like coarse steel and the narrow grooves like the cleft of a misshapen fruit and the little specks of flint that a fingernail could pull away from their bed, and tried to imagine what the place, as a whole, was like.

The memory of colour and light still remains with me, and even now there are moments at which my mind, stimulated by some poignant association with my earlier life, will break unexpectedly into a brilliance of images capable of leaving me breathless and dazed. But I have worked hard to eradicate visual imagination in myself. It has been necessary to do so in order to be more wholly free of a seeing past which is just so much dead weight on my life and which could only torment me if I indulged it. At ordinary times now the effect to recapture colours and effects of light is laborious and painful to me. And here on the granite outcropping in the middle of Rose Gwavas heath I could set in the sky no more than a wan, infinitely aged moon like a crater burnt out centuries ago, casting no light, and the weird, druidical forms around me were rather felt as presences than seen. They held up their arms and crazy, garlanded heads towards the moon, but there was no light glinting on the blade of the knife, and there was no sacrifice but only the ghost of a rite without meaning. And then I remembered.

'There isn't a moon up,' Mrs. Nance had said.

And the knowledge of that restored me. The darkness around me was more than the darkness of my mind. What little I had conjured up for colour and light was more intense than to-night's reality. I was the master. This dull, hesitant moon was part of my creation, and if the blood of the sacrifice did not flow in my mind it flowed even less and was not even suggested in the desolate theatre of solid granite on which I stood.

I let it all die out of me and lived again in the actual, simple world of my own senses. This was a garden attached to a human dwelling. Its realities of massiveness and the scents of the night I could savour as precisely as any man alive.

And the sounds, too.

As I stood here I heard not far away in what must have been deep woods, to judge by the echo, the flurry of a squealing rabbit and after that triumphant hooting from an owl which was joined at once by another, no doubt its mate. In the deep silence that followed there was a fox coughing and what sounded like the grunt of a badger. The wings of a bat were busy in the air above my head. Here and in every part of the night silence was

20

an illusion. If I walked out past the nearest farmstead I should hear the restlessness of cattle thudding against their stalls. And all this was reality. It was alive, and it was in my world by natural right and without my effort.

For a moment the sense of labour, discomfort and loss returned. I began to wonder about the girl Sophie Madron and to indulge a hope that she might come out here and be near me in the darkness with her dark, shadowy scent. I would allow myself a little insincerity and pretend that I needed a guiding hand in climbing presently down from these rocks. That would help me to begin to defeat her remoteness.

She was not coming out, though. And I could not wait here long enough to coerce her mind from a distance. The air was turning chilly.

I fancied Sophie in the drawing-room, reading a book or stretched out on a divan, smoking a cigarette and thinking of nothing more substantial than the smoke of a cigarette. And that roused again for a moment the nostalgia of sight. I had definite memories of lighted rooms seen from the darkness outside. I was troubled by the image of an uncurtained window behind which a woman sat drowsily looking up from the pages of a book and then returning to it in complete ignorance of the watcher. That image died out, and I was left with the thought that this girl Sophie Madron was probably not in the house at all, but out with a young man called Nicky Polgigga of whom I had no cognizance and walking in a direction that I could not possibly know.

The thought displeased me.

But it was wrong. Sophie was there in the house. I heard from closer than I had supposed the shifting of a piece of furniture, then little, indistinct sounds and then the scratching of a gramophone needle, and now music coming out to me through an open window. It was music for a small orchestra by one of the moderns, Auric or Milhaud or some unimportant Stravinsky trifle, slick and intelligent music without superfluous weight. I liked it. And I liked even more the simple fact that, although she did not know it, Sophie Madron was contriving to afford me pleasure by what she was doing.

I listened to the end of the record, waited for a moment to hear if any other records were to be played and then decided that it was too chilly to stay out any longer. I wondered whether to join Sophie and possibly sit up talking with her for a while. I decided not to. I was feeling now sufficiently at ease with the environment of Rose Gwavas not to suffer any anxiety to force a contact which was not immediately forthcoming. I could wait. I tapped my way to the edge of the granite, let myself carefully down and walked round the end of the house to the door at which I had come out. My fingers in locating the door found themselves among the little, polished leaves of a shrub growing under the cornice. I crushed two or three of the leaves, and the fine, aromatic fragrance of myrtle rose up into my nostrils.

CHAPTER TWO

MRS. NANCE HAD a magnificent pair of legs on her. It was a pleasure to thump them. I kneaded and hacked. I pounded. I beat. It gave her pleasure and release. She breathed deeply and lifted up the great weight of her thighs voluptuously like a cat stretching. When I had finished she put up a hand and ruffled my hair, and we laughed at each other.

It was like that. No question about it. An element of erotic delight entered into the process and lay quite definitely there in the heart of the relationship between Mrs. Nance and myself. And to some people the fact will seem an obscene one. I do not find it so. At any rate I did not find it so with Mrs. Nance. I have treated old ladies in South Kensington hotels with whom it was obscene. And it was obscene with them because the general, diffuse and unacknowledged itch they contrived to gratify here and there in the ministrations of a masseur, in the conversation of curates and in discovering the misbehaviour of young people alike was something which they themselves would have thought obscene if it could have been explained to them. Not so with Mrs. Nance. Mrs. Nance had self-knowledge and recognised herself for a woman playing a rôle more male than female in which there was little scope for erotic relationships of a normal kind except with men who, like the husband who had at length run away from her in order at length to be himself (that is, to be what other people thought that every man without discrimination of persons should be), had been created for a rôle more female than male.

I do not feel capable of estimating to what extent the partial paralysis which Mrs. Nance had developed was neurotic and to be thought of as the product of a desire of the mind. I am not, in fact, at all convinced about distinctions between the physical and the mental and cannot therefore quite understand how a physical condition should be induced by a non-physical disturbance any more than I can understand how the fantasy creation of great art may be thought to be caused by a failure in the normal processes of digestion. I am aware of the human being as a creature of only half-realised potentialities which I can only think it a conceit of the intelligence to claim to have once and for all understood.

Mrs. Nance would herself have admitted, for purposes of conversation, that her ailment was neurotic and was even capable of seeing that it fitted into the general pattern of an extreme imitation of her father and a transference to herself of a great many characteristics which his friends would have thought of as rightly belonging to Admiral Madron and to no other person. But is this, in fact, an explanation? The simple truth of the matter was that Mrs. Nance suffered from an extremely painful affection of the hips and thighs which excluded her from most of the activities she had formerly delighted in and of which she would have been extremely glad to be rid.

If the alleviation of this pain gave her delight of the kind that is thought of as erotic and of the kind for which her nature robbed her of more normal expressions and if the person whose manipulation of her nerves gave her this delight became therein a friend so necessary to her that she could think of him as a lover—well, that may have been perverse, and it may have been abnormal, but it was also a source of reliable and deep contentment in the lives of two people.

I have come across relationships between people which have revolted me. And these have been relationships of a sexually direct and normal kind. Nor have they always been the relationships of young men with middle-aged women or the reverse. They have been simply those apparent marriages in which the proper and, as it were, the institutional act of marriage has been anything other than the obvious and spontaneous commerce between two people whose purposes with each other were total and absolute.

Therefore I say Mrs. Nance had a magnificent pair of legs on her which it was a pleasure to thump and that I thumped them with pleasure, kneaded and hacked, pounded and beat, with *pétrissage* and no less with *effleurage,* and that Mrs. Nance received the treatment voluptuously and at the end of it turned over the weight of her thighs with all the languor of a great cat and put up a hand and ruffled my hair, and that we laughed at each other then like a pair of lovers returning to wakefulness. It seemed all right to me. True, my ethics are purely empirical. I am one of those who labour perpetually at a disadvantage. And therefore I, like the poor, can do no wrong—except to myself. Only, this morning I felt a little more self-conscious about my occupation than is usual with me.

I had awakened with Sophie Madron as the waking thought in my head. It was a genuine and particular interest, then. It survived the infiltration of a good night's rest. It was not merely the general tendency in arriving at a new destination to seize upon the first delightful object that presents itself and cling to it.

And I wondered. I could very well imagine the young people criticising their aunt, before I came, for wanting her masseur to come and stay down here in the house. It would seem to them an indulgence of the wrong kind. And while the polite and manly John would dismiss the thought with a laugh at Auntie's oddities and a psychological wisecrack, Sophie would treat it seriously. I fancied her distaste. I had come across it before in the young dancers from the ballet schools who are a main stand-by, though by no means the deepest source of income, in my London practice. I had so often found the taut young limbs, the ankles and thighs of these highly fastidious and at the same time highly passionate young women offer resistance to my treatment and in consequence rob themselves of half its good effect. I have fancied that the reason for this resistance lay in their feeling that all tactile pleasure belonged either to the dance itself or to love and that anything which came between the two was in some sense a defloration and intolerable. In older and less fastidious women this thought has often led to crazy advances on their part. But the young dancers I have found to be a curious mixture of extreme frankness and

26

essential purity of heart. And from the little I knew and the more that her aunt had told me I thought that the temperament I detected in Sophie Madron was precisely this dancer's temperament. There is, I suppose, something so inevitable, so intimate and melodramatically right, in the rôle of a blind masseur that in the eyes of self-conscious people it is either intolerable, metaphysical virtue or naked obscenity.

The conflict was here too. Sophie was a creature of passionate candour, veiled by a too sensitive, questioning diffidence. And until she had me in focus as a person fit for the assumption of a delicate rôle she could not so much as bring herself to shake hands with me. On a more prolonged acquaintance her distaste might suddenly lift. Or it might only deepen. In the meantime she was no doubt labouring under the difficulty of convincing herself that Mrs. Nance was my patient and my friend and that our relationship was to be seen in the same objective light as any other.

I thought it out thus while Mrs. Nance dressed and I sat on the edge of the bed smoking a cigarette. A prolonged massage momentarily exhausts me, and I find a cigarette helpful. At other times I have the notion that tobacco smoke dulls all my senses, but especially those of taste and smell, and will only smoke a cigarette when some other powerful taste like that of coffee accompanies it.

But I may be wrong. All these ideas of Sophie Madron may have been wrong. And I may be at fault in the whole deliberate structure of a life that I have built around myself and my limitations.

I smoked my cigarette. Mrs. Nance dressed. I got up to go. Mrs. Nance had something to say.

She hoped I would go out with her young people to-day while she painted five tulips in a lustre bowl.

And then she said:

'Amity Nance lives at Falmouth, Louis. I told you we had a little cousin who's blind. . . .'

'Yes. . . .'

And I didn't want to hear. I pretended to be stupid.

'. . . Yes, I remember.'

'. . . She lives up there at Falmouth with her teacher.'

I did not wish to be implicated. I remembered well enough. Amity Nance was blind from birth. I seemed to remember that she was deaf or mute into the bargain. Or both, indeed. I repelled the thought of other people's infirmities, especially when they were greater than my own. It was a call on my emotions, and it was prematurely made. I did not wish to be implicated.

'Of course, yes. You told me. A remarkable case, you said. . . .'

I would not respond. I would not. And I went out of Mrs. Nance's room with a disturbed mind. I feel that I have less control over my face than other people. It is difficult to lie or conceal your feelings when you cannot watch the expression on another person's face. I may have blushed or puckered my forehead. I cannot tell. And I went out of the room full of a shameful irritation and wishing I could open my eyes before a mirror and see my own face once before I closed them again.

It was hot enough by eleven o'clock to sit out on the

lawn. I had books with me and read intermittently. John had found me the books. He said there were braille books in the house if I cared to examine them. As a matter of fact they were quite new. Mrs. Nance had evidently written up to the National Institute for the Blind and got a catalogue and chosen out those I might have some use for among the new publications. Most of them I already had, and the rest were not exciting. I could be interested in Talleyrand but not in Mr. Duff Cooper except as an anthropological specimen. There were also contemporary poets or at any rate that gentle, sad man T. S. Eliot. And there was *Thus Spake Zarathustra.* I think it is amusing to read about the Superman in braille, so I had *Thus Spake Zarathustra.* But I only played about among the dimpled pages and made no pretence of studying except when I heard the girl Betty des Voeux come out on the lawn with John and a friend of theirs whose voice was as metallic as her own though male.

John had the *Radio Times* in braille. He said it had just come.

Betty des Voeux thought it interesting that I should be reading with my fingers. She had heard about the braille alphabet at school. She wanted to look.

'Isn't it remarkable,' she said, 'what they can do for people now? But I'm sure I should never be clever enough. It would all be wasted on me.'

She rubbed her vigorous, inept fingers over the page.

'Is it in the same direction as ours? I mean,' she said, 'the Chinese read upwards and from left to right. Oh, dear. . . .'

She stood up and said they really had better get off home for lunch. What were the arrangements now for the afternoon? They thought of going off to Pengenno Cove on the other side of the bay for a swim. Did I feel inclined to? Oh, here was Sophie.

'Sophie, darling. Are you coming for a swim this afternoon? Or would you . . .'

I hoped Sophie would refuse. Then I would hold back too, and there might be the chance of having Sophie to herself. I would not go in the sea myself in any case. I swim well and like the cold April water, but I do not like to swim with people until I know them well because I must often swim close to them and be guided by their movements. It is a peculiar kind of intimacy. And certainly the thought of sitting on the beach guarding their clothes while four other people went in to swim was not attractive. Particularly did I dislike the thought of Sophie Madron leaving me there on the beach in a kind of old woman's posture while she fled away from my helplessness and took the slender, dark excitement that I could not even yet picture to myself joyously into the strangeness of the sea. It would bring back to me the feeling of incapacity that I had felt as an adolescent when somebody two or three years my senior walked off with the girl I had fancied myself in love with. The feelings of adolescence are extremely painful when they recur in the male adult. I hoped that Sophie would not go for a swim this afternoon.

Later, I thought, she can swim with me. Not now, with these immature but horribly self-confident people. Later, with me.

I need not have worried.

'I thought of walking out beyond Kingdom Come,' she said. 'I don't know whether Mr. Dunkel. . . . I thought you might not want to bathe, Mr. Dunkel. In which case . . .'

'It will be cold,' I said, 'in April.'

And Betty des Voeux sounded relieved.

'Yes, it might, if you don't swim all the year round, I suppose.'

'Well, then . . .' said John.

' I should like to walk inland,' I said, 'and learn my way about more.'

And that was settled.

I supposed that Sophie's invitation had emanated as a secret order from upstairs. Mrs. Nance had probably suggested to her that I ought to be saved from the company of Betty des Voeux and John's other friends of the same type as much as possible, and Mrs. Nance's suggestions had a way of being put into action. But I did not mind that.

Sophie was detached and if I may put it so anæsthetic. From the charming and natural way in which she talked about the country-side and the people in it I could have imagined that a sweet-natured, prim little schoolmistress was walking beside me.

Only once was there any hint of passion, and that vanished as quickly as it came.

We walked out over Rose Gwavas heath to get to the Land's End road. At first Sophie walked with exaggerated slowness, but she soon found that I followed her movements by instinct and kept the brambles away quite easily with the stick I had brought and only needed telling of obstructions that hung over the path or grew across it breast high, and her reaction to the discovery was to become more unrestrained in every way. She pointed out objects on the way, always with a little hesitation as if she had to make up her mind first that I should not resent being told, or as if she wanted to be sure before she spoke that she could describe what she saw accurately enough for me to understand. That hesitation also disappeared after a while, and she talked quite freely of the prehistoric quoits and the logan stones and the flowers that grew around and the legends attached to particular hollows and mounds and farmsteads.

She did not tell me until we had left the heath and come out on the Land's End road that adders had been lying out, basking on the whins as we passed. I laughed at her. Her voice was half-apologetic and half-defiant.

'It would have fidgeted me, anyway,' she said.

And then she explained the point of coming out in this direction. There was a farm called Chy Tralee, just out beyond Kingdom Come, and she had a bull-terrier bitch there. Her aunt had decided she didn't want it about the house, and so she had got Mrs. Tralee to keep it at the farm for her.

'Mrs. Tralee's a very great friend of mine,' she said, 'and Chy Tralee's a lovely farm. I like farms. And we can have tea there.'

She didn't ask me whether I liked farms or not. I took it as a compliment.

'But what about Mrs. Nance? I should have thought...'

'I know. She did have a bloodhound once, but she got tired of it. That was when I got Jess. I think I got Jess partly to protect me against the bloodhound. It was a terrifying creature to have about the house.'

'Yes, I suppose one Admiral's enough at a time.'

'Oh, you've noticed? Yes. Anyway, Jess is at Chy Tralee now. She's just got pups.'

'Proper ones?'

'Yes, I bred them. I had her properly mated. Is that. . . is it an awful daddy's girl kind of thing to do? Anyway, Jess has got pups now, and they're lovely things. I think so, anyway.'

And I imagined her blushing. I was puzzled. This was all very ingenuous and unlike the vague idea of Sophie Madron that I had begun to cultivate. It might almost have been a game, I thought, to draw me out. Only not quite. Or it might have been a quite spontaneous reflection of what Sophie Madron felt about me. I suppose it is natural for people to regard a blind man as in some way more innocent than other men and requiring to be presented with personal values that are simplified—as one regards a foreigner who has difficulty with the language. Only not with Sophie Madron. No, it was some kind of game with her. It was her way of both shying at me and being nice at the same time. It might quite well be unconscious and as it were instinctive nevertheless.

We came to the farm. I did like farms, though I fancy my reasons were rather less sentimental than those that Sophie had persuaded herself into and cultivated. It is the sublime inconsequence of a farm that I like, the confusion of noises, the sense of unreality that is given as a great and heavenly gift to human beings who live among thudding, moaning cattle, and tumbling milk-cans, and hens screeching underfoot and who, no matter how they try, can never coerce their lives into routine, but must always wait on the weather and market prices and the temperamental vagaries of their stock, and at one time spend idle weeks in the rain, and at another toil both day and night, and at yet another time waste precious hours chasing a cow which has got into the wrong field and which, in running away, impales itself eventually on the railings, or in segregating cock chickens of three weeks old who suddenly discover their sex and in one afternoon reduce each other to bleeding wisps of tow. That is what I like about a farm. What excited Sophie at this time was, I fancy, the sense of surging life and fertility and simple, earthy values and all those things about which immature and puffy minds so easily grow lyrical.

Only I believe that this, too, was with Sophie a bit of a game—which she played with herself. And as a matter of fact the single hint she gave of genuine passion this afternoon was given at the height of an attack of precisely this fertility lyricism.

The bitch Jess did not come up to greet Sophie as we entered the yard. Jess was too busy with her pups. Sophie led me to where she was standing, holding, I remember, only the stuff of my sleeve. Jess let me caress her, as all animals do. She was a noble creature, swollen with milk, but with that tautness of limb and muscle that bull-terriers have so much more perfectly than other dogs (and which again made me think of the ballet and of the limbs of the male dancers). As I ran my hand along Jess's back I could feel the tug of the pups at her nipples below. I did not dare to touch her there.

'There are seven of them,' Sophie said. 'Oh, look . . .'

I could not look.

'. . . She's walked off, and they're all tumbling away from her. One of them's hanging on and being dragged along the ground. Oh, I wish you could see.'

A girl came up to us who was Mrs. Tralee's daughter, a girl with very strong hands and a deep, cynical voice. I wondered if she might be the cause of Sophie Madron's mood this afternoon, a suspicion of Lesbian attachment, perhaps, but I decided not.

They were calving up in the cart bay, the Tralee girl told us. Sophie wanted to see that. We went and stood among a great deal of straw.

'How she suffers,' said Sophie.

''Tis the first calf. A heifer's calf.'

'The way she's twisted up,' said Sophie. 'All twisted up, as if she had a knife in her. . . . What's Ken doing?'

'He's got to break the skin. It's the way with a young cow. Look now. There's the feet come. They'll have to put a rope round the feet now and pull. It'll take all three of they, lying on the ground too.'

Sophie was trembling. She was standing close enough for me to feel her clench herself and tremble with anguish for the cow's pain. I hated that. It was the wrong kind of sympathy, the kind a commonplace woman feels. And then she changed and was perfectly still, watching, I knew, in simple, passionate watchfulness. There was no more of the awful, spinsterly flutter. And now it was my turn. The depth of this stillness in Sophie was such as to make me tremble. It was true, ice-cold passion. She was feeling all the cow's pain and yet remained quite still and apathetic through it now. This was not the stolid, unimaginative apathy of the farm girl. It was that infinite, passionate sympathy which has no trace in it of what is called womanly. I thrilled to it as if it were something I had reason to be proud of myself. The cow was moaning. And I wanted to laugh with pleasure.

A single last vibration passed through Sophie's frame, and I knew the calf was born. The men, three of them, had dragged the cow from one end of the cart bay to the other in getting the calf away. Now it was born, and that was all over.

'It looks dead,' said Sophie, with a strange, dead coldness in her voice.

But the men were slapping the calf with the palms of their hands, and the farm girl muttered that it was alive all right and left us, I suppose, to tend the calf and put it on straw up against its mother.

We went into the big farm kitchen. Mrs. Tralee had the tea ready. She was a heavy woman, who moved about with difficulty. With her and with the three sons who presently came in one after the other Sophie reverted to the tones of girlish over-appreciation for a few minutes and then was silent throughout the meal, which was a hearty one, with splits and scalded cream, jam and saffron cake and three cold pasties.

But I was satisfied.

After the meal we walked all over the farm, through

the orchards, with the faint, shrill scent of the late blossom, and through the deepening hay-fields where I tasted the young, acid sorrel, and among the stinking pigs and the sweet cows which were being milked by some new electrical means which I did not quite understand except that I suppose vibration was set up in the metal tubes fitted to their udders. Some of the cows would not take these metal tubes and still had to be milked by hand. Where the Chy Tralee land reached out over the sea it was divided up into little patches of field which grew in rotation potatoes and flowers, daffodils, narcissi, anemones. The daughter of the farm walked with us. We left her at the most seaward point of the land and cut across somebody else's fields to reach a tiny hamlet two miles outside Kingdom Come. This hamlet possessed an attractive pub. with low ceilings and cobbled floors and an open fire with corner seats.

Sophie had only brought me here, I thought, in order to fulfil her duty of showing me round the neighbourhood, for she remained silent and was as utterly remote from me as on our first encounter. I think she felt that she had behaved mistakenly and perhaps, if my guesses were right, that she could not dodge me by playing the sweet and unsuspecting, warm-hearted schoolmistress. It was not so pleasant as it might have been sitting together in the pub. here, each with a load of private speculation inside. Sophie must have been irritated. I should have been irritated myself, but for the fact that I fancied I understood why irritation might be present and was thereby freed of it. As it was I felt deeply subdued.

There was one more effort made on Sophie's part. It was a trial of the approach direct.

'Do you mind not being able to see?'

But I wasn't going to be the first to make confessions.

'Now and then,' I said. 'Not very much. I gather from other people's conversation what they see, and I don't often feel that I'm missing much.'

'I see. . . .'

And that was not so far from a declaration of war.

It was left at that, and I was rather glad. When things begin to happen too quickly I am liable to be left far behind.

John was out to dinner. Sophie and Mrs. Nance and I had dinner together in a smaller room and with candles. Every now and then, when the door was opened or when anybody stretched across the table, I could feel the hot air over the candles wafted into my face. It was very quiet and intimate. Nobody said anything worthy of attention. I listened to the voices of the two women and not their words. Mrs. Nance's voice was rich and full, with a certain male slanginess of the kind that is rarely found in men. It was in its way an obvious voice. Sophie's, on the other hand, was so vague that it would always be difficult to recall it in her absence. It changed from moment to moment and showed, as they say, no marked characteristics at all. There was a faint burr in it which, I suppose, was partly Cornish and partly Middle West, but most of the time this was quite imperceptible. At moments there was a vibrant headiness musical enough for any ear, but except at those moments it was a cold voice, toneless, and one in which the phonetician would have been completely uninterested.

It was, in fact, the voice of a woman fluid as water, of a nature untapped and still to be roused and stirred into wakefulness.

And yet with a readiness for the moment as it came that made this afternoon's mood seem comically out of its setting. Sophie at dinner was quietly suave and agreeable both with Mrs. Nance and with me. After supper she disappeared, while I was with Mrs. Nance in the library, and it was certain enough where she had gone. I minded not at all. Especially after more of the good port it was almost luxurious to inform oneself that everything must be allowed to happen in its own good time and that the sooner young men called Nicky Polgigga were allowed to complete the dissatisfaction of young women called Sophie Madron the better it would be for everybody concerned.

But there was something to worry about.

I went out of the house and over the lawn and through an avenue of beeches to the water garden. It was difficult and uneven ground, and the problem of finding my way to a little bridge over the lily pond was sufficient to occupy me for a while. And then I was free to lean on the parapet of smooth cherry wood and breathe in the damp, faintly enervating sweetness and to take out the worrying thought of Amity Nance from the back of my mind and examine it.

Mrs. Nance evidently wanted to have Amity Nance staying down here with me. Her thought was presumably that we should 'have something in common.' And suppose we had? It was not something that we wanted to talk about. In fact, of all things on the earth it was the one thing I could definitely say I was not interested in. Whether my own or somebody else's, blindness was plainly and flatly unwelcome to me. It was as unwelcome as the meaningless noises of London streets or the self-importance of politically minded young people who marched in bands through those streets shouting their slogans or as the attentions of an unattractive woman. And what nonsense it was to think that to 'have something in common' is a happy bond between two people. I have never found that young men who grew beards were particularly happy to come face to face with other young men similarly bearded. On the contrary. And I have been present at highly embarrassing evening functions when two women dressed in the same exclusive Paris model were presented to each other. It was plain, flat nonsense. It was such very plain, flat nonsense, in fact, that it couldn't be the thought in Mrs. Nance's head. Mrs Nance was not so inept, so hopelessly amateur.

I did not care to speculate on what her thought was, so long as I could be convinced about what it wasn't. So long as Mrs. Nance wasn't imperilling our relationship by demonstrating this particular stupidity I didn't mind her wanting to make use of me in the development of Amity Nance's educational processes or even fancying, on the other hand, that to know Amity Nance might be a help to me in some way. That was her business, and she would reveal it in time.

But I was going to resist. I hadn't room in my world for other people's disabilities. I have won my own integrity, or what I thought of rather as my own sophistication, at the cost of a great deal of struggle and anxiety and painful working upon myself to eradicate one thing and fortify another and leave myself neither bitter nor piteously resigned. In many ways the struggle still went on at that time. I had, I thought, a deeper sanity and rather more personal strength than most of the people I came across, but the difficulties remained, and I had to labour, labour to be fully human, labour against the awful passivity which I have found in other blind people who, with all their charm and intelligence, had stepped down from the fully human level to the level of pious institutions. I did not propose to risk disturbance of all that I had contrived in and for myself.

It would have been different if I had been securely lodged at that moment or free of all other human entanglements whatever. For instance, if there had been no other object of interest for me at Rose Gwavas, no other matter to be slowly broached and painstakingly adjusted.

No, I would let Mrs. Nance's intentions in the matter of Amity Nance die of a lack of response.

I stared out over the lily pond and into the depth of the willow shadows beyond. That is the only way I can put it. I stared. It was a kind of yearning outward of all the senses, a powerful listlessness, a heavy, eyeless staring which brought into play the muscles about the sockets of my late, lamented eyes and made them ache for a moment. There was nothing audible but a movement of water so light that it may only have taken place in the imagination and farther away the sound of what may have been cricket or grasshopper or a nested bird turning in its sleep. The silence was presently disturbed by the mewing of a kitten. It came up to me. I put my hand down to the arched, slender back and the tense, erect tail and remembered hearing Sophie talking to a kitten yesterday evening just after my arrival. The kitten mewed around me and pressed itself this way and that against my leg. I had no doubt interrupted its juvenile hunting. It ought not to be out. There were too many owls around here. As I caressed the kitten an owl came hooting through the trees and broke the comfortable depth of the silence.

But I would not interrupt the courses of things. To attempt to take the kitten indoors would be a bad, sentimental, anthropomorphic kindness and a sickness of nature. I would let it hunt, and if it crossed the path of an owl I would allow myself to be sorry, but I would not interfere and would not try now to introduce the element of security into a life by its nature insecure.

Nor would I lay myself out to be the instrument of other people's kindnesses. I returned to the previous thought. If Mrs. Nance wanted Amity Nance to come down here, let her arrange it and not try to make me responsible by a previous assent.

I would not seek to be reminded. It is not a good thing to be forced into consciousness of the nature of one's disability.

And with Amity Nance it would be continuous, obsessive consciousness. The thought of her was accompanied by thoughts of all the cumbrous and humiliating apparatus for the blind which I had exerted myself very strenuously to avoid, all the chiming watches, trained dogs and braille typewriters whose only purpose, so far as I can understand, is to turn the human being into a subject for demonstrations of popular science. Amity Nance was one of those people whose pathos is so obvious that they appear in the newspapers as human interest stories and whose doings are chronicled in the *New Beacon* to be a light and an encouragement to 'their fellow sightless ones.' Mrs. Nance had mentioned the child to me before, but I remembered her name chiefly from a home-page article which some woman had once insisted on reading aloud to me in a railway carriage, asking me if I knew her. This article spoke of the self-sacrifice of the teacher who had 'devoted her life' to Amity Nance and of mind triumphing over matter and of the miracles of science and of a cheerfulness in affliction which must be a consolation to millions in their daily lives. There was something quite unspeakable about it. Certainly it was not the fault of Amity Nance, but the odour was there, a blindness kept so much in the sun that it could be smelt, an awful, antiseptic odour like that of a nursing-home.

My feelings about it did not perhaps do me credit, but they were my feelings. And I have learnt the virtue of not pretending to feelings which I have not and ought to have. I will not lay claim to an altruism of which I am not guilty. Only, there was another side. And I wondered. There might be a resistance of precisely this kind in Sophie Madron's attitude towards myself. And it might be more inhibiting to her than all the subtler inhibitions by which I had tried this morning to account for aloofness in her. It might be that I was laying up trouble for myself by permitting myself to be so much as ordinarily interested.

The mere consciousness of physical pain or loss is repellent to physically sensitive people.

I thought of the young dancers from the ballet schools again. I have a habit when I am doing nothing else of stretching my finger joints and making them crack. It is something that I was told to do by my first piano teacher, and I have never rid myself of the habit.

I have cracked my fingers thus when I have been sitting with dancers, and they have winced and drawn in their breath with apprehension and asked me not to do it again. Yet they are people who themselves will break a toe or tear a muscle with perfect equanimity. And it was conceivable that to Sophie Madron this automatic fear of mutilation and her quite spontaneous turning away from a physically imperfect man were stronger in her than any common pity or particular friendliness.

The same impulse works in ways opposite to each other. Women with a rare taste in sensation have been brought into my arms by precisely that fear of mutilation which another woman turns away from. And this is a fact which has pleased me only in ironical, vicious moods. I prefer on the whole not to be a creature possessed of a horrible fascination, not to be an exotic taste, a caviare, and in competition with the all-in wrestler, the negro gigolo and that favourite lover of many pampered women whose main attraction is that he does not wash.

I thought of these things and indulged my capacity for desolation and partly hoped that Sophie Madron would indeed turn away from me.

But it was April, and the air turned chilly. I went into the house and up to my room. I plucked off leaves of the myrtle as I went in, for I am conscious of the necessity of developing little, personal rituals. I crushed them for the scent and as I undressed laid them on my dressing table, feeling the night air cold on the back of my hand, coming through the open window where a leafing but as yet unflowering jasmine clustered over the sill and rustled faintly all night. It was a matter of hours before I could sleep. The chiming of both the church towers of Trevillian and Kingdom Come reached me faintly across the open heath, not quite in time with each other. The moment I dozed off I was plagued in sleep with the anguish of reminiscence which immediately awoke me and left me lying hot and restless and dark in mind.

CHAPTER THREE

MY FATHER WAS a stern man, and I did not like to tell him. I knew what he would say. He would look thoughtful and even a little annoyed, weighing the expense against the gravity of the situation, and after chewing his moustache two or three times he would say, 'Well, you'd better go and see Harry Tyas. I'll give you a note.' And then he would go out of the room.

This would in some ways be the worst part of it all. 'You'd better...' always gave me terrible feelings. 'You'd better . . . better go and tell your mother you're sorry . . . better stop reading now, lad, and get off to bed . . . better go into town and call at the office for it . . . better not let me hear you say that again, lad. . . .' It was a phrase that always had the same echoes and always gave me the same feelings of awful discouragement lightly tinged with guilt. 'You'd better. . . .' It was a phrase of concealment, a phrase behind which my father concealed his real meaning in a grave situation. It stood for all the inaccessibility of adult life and all the weighty responsibilities, which I was not allowed to understand, though one day they would be mine too. 'You'd better . . .' It was always said in a grave impersonal voice, and it tyrannised over me and made me feel worthless and ashamed more than any other phrase could.

It was this phrase that I could not face. I wanted a display of feeling. I wanted to know what my father really felt about it. And he would not tell me.

Then to go down to Harry Tyas with a note. . . . Harry Tyas was the optician. He was a little man with an inquisitive face who spoke in a broad, Yorkshire voice. My father liked him. So did other people. He was a J.P. like my father. But I knew my mother hated him. I think it was partly because of his Yorkshire accent but more because of the fact that my father met him to go down to the Masons' Lodge and the way he came to smoke a cigar and drink a glass of whisky with my father in her drawing-room and took no notice of her. I found him sinister for the same reason I suppose—because he was my father's intimate in a world from which I was excluded. And it depressed me to pass his shop on the way to school and to see the optical instruments and charts and photographs of pretty women wearing spectacles in the window and the name H. W. Tyas written above, and the elegance of the shop, which was in the best part of Norwich, and the way the man's face would light up with amusement if I spoke to him as I passed when he was chatting with a well-dressed customer in the doorway of the shop.

I could not imagine what would take place in that shop when I went into it with a note from my father. All I knew was that I should emerge from it wearing glasses.

And that I should have to walk through Norwich wearing glasses and then take a tram out to school and walk through the gates and into the quadrangle and that nobody would be there except perhaps the caretaker and a boy from one of the lower forms going to the lavatory, or a prefect carrying a message, and that then I should go upstairs, along the corridors, into my own form-room, and present another note to the master who was taking the form, and stand there by his desk while he read it and marked my name in the register, and all the other boys nudged each other and whispered about my specs, and that from this moment onward everbody's attitude to me would be changed. . . . For the boys who wore glasses were a different species, like the boarders. One or two who were very reckless and good at games had managed to mix in properly with the other boys, but most of them were quiet, shy people who stood in a group by themselves at break and always worked very hard in school and never cheeked the masters, and had pure minds, and did not laugh except in a quiet, shy way. I did not wish to be one of them. It wasn't that I hated them. I sometimes made friends with one or another of them on the quiet. They talked more sensibly about a lot of things, and they were kind, like women. I did not want to be one of them because they were special and separate, and I wanted to be like everybody else and a bit more active than most.

Besides, I was just beginning to care about how I looked. I had been allowed to choose my own cloth for the last two new suits I had, and I had bought a walking stick for walking out on Sunday with. Two or three of us strolled up and down in the park on Sunday afternoons and talked to girls whom one or another of us knew. As a matter of fact, although I was shy myself and would not go out with them after church in the evening, I knew that some of the girls quite liked me and would probably have let me kiss them if I had tried to. I had rather nice, thick hair with a natural wave in it, and my father always liked me to have good clothes.

And so I didn't say anything. Sometimes it wasn't so bad, and then I told myself that it was only doing too much reading that caused the pains and that when I left school it would be all right, if not before. When the pains were coming on I thought all kinds of romantic thoughts about the suffering I had to undergo in my life. And when they were at their worst I was too dazed to think anything at all, and only prayed to be allowed to die or even to go to sleep. We were doing *King John* at school, and that helped me quite a lot. I used to keep my finger in Act IV, Scene I, and keep glancing back and forward to it in class. It was marvellous the way Hubert de Burgh and Arthur went on arguing in poetry about whether Arthur should have his eyes burnt out or not, and it looked certain that Hubert de Burgh would have the best of the argument. Arthur was pleading now. He was in tears.

> . . . *Hubert,* if you will cut out my tongue,
> So I may keepe mine eyes. O fpare mine eyes,
> Though to no vfe but ftill to looke on you. . . .

It was terribly real. I could hear the voice of Hubert de Burgh's refusal spoken again somewhere not in the book at all, but in the air outside me.

> Come Boy prepare your felfe.

49

And I could feel the red-hot irons approaching and the heat from them scorching my face. It was like that. And then it was all over, and I didn't mind the pains. Quite unexpectedly Hubert de Burgh changed his mind and let the irons cool and went out with Arthur, promising to look after him. It was so real that I almost wept in class, and once I gulped so loud that the English master fetched me out in front and asked me what I'd been talking about, and when I said nothing, sent me out of the room.

At last my father noticed. I was very pale and tired, and my eyelids were red. He questioned me and was very sympathetic, though he said I ought to have told him at first, and said he'd arrange with Harry Tyas. And it wasn't anything like so bad as I had expected.

It was unpleasant having my eyes tested, and I nearly fainted with having a light shone into them and all the apparatus arranged in front of me. But as a matter of fact Harry Tyas was very decent and made no jokes at all, but just explained things to me very interestingly and told me to say when I wanted to rest my eyes for a minute. It had been a false alarm. I was getting a bit long-sighted, that was all. It was just eye-strain, and if I wore my glasses all the time for a fortnight I could then use them only for close work and not have to wear them outside at all. Even that fortnight was nothing, because I had to wait three or four days for the lenses to be fitted, and so had plenty of time to tell the boys at school all about it beforehand and forestall their whispering and laughing when I turned up at last with my glasses on.

I was nearly seventeen at the time, and it was all fixed

up that I should go to London University to do medicine at the end of another school year.

At a later period too I made use of one of W. Shakespeare's plays.

This time it was *The Tragicall Hiftorie of Hamlet Prince of Denmark.*

It was Act III, Scene III. I have listened to it being played in the theatre many times since, and it has never quite failed me, though now it is worn transparently thin.

Prince Hamlet was coming down the stairs on his way to see his mother. At the foot of the stairs was that King Claudius, his uncle, who had murdered his father, King Hamlet, and married Queen Gertrude his mother—this the cause of Prince Hamlet's disordered mind. And King Claudius was kneeling at a faldstool in the attitude of prayer.

In a flash Prince Hamlet's sword was half out of its scabbard.

But let me turn back and recapture King Claudius' language of remorse before he knelt.

He was saying:

O my offence is ranck, it fmels to heauen,
It hath the primall eldeft curfe vppont,
A brothers murther, pray can I not,
Though inclination be as fharp as will,
My ftronger guilt defeats my ftrong entent,
And like a man to double bufsines bound,
I ftand in pause where I fhall firft beginne,
And both neglect, what if this curfed hand
Were thicker than it felfe with brothers blood,

Is there not raine enough in the fweete Heauens
To wafh it white as fnowe, whereto ferues mercy
But to confront the vifage of offence?
And what's in prayer but this two fold force,
To be foreftalled ere we come to fall,
Or pardond being downe, then I'le looke up.
My fault is paft, but oh what forme of prayer
Can ferve my turne, forgiue me my foule murther,
That cannot be fince I am ftill poffeft
Of thofe effects for which I did the murther;
My Crowne, mine owne ambition, and my Queene;
May one be pardond and retaine the offence?
In the corrupted currents of this world,
Offences guilded hand may fhoue by iustice,
And oft tis feene the wicked prize it felfe
Buyes out the law, but tis not fo aboue,
There is no fhufling, there the action lies
In his true nature, and we our felues compeld
Euen to the teeth and forhead of our faults
To giue in euidence, what then, what refts,
Try what repentance can, what can it not,
Yet what can it, when one cannot repent?
O wretched ftate, ô bofome black as death,
O limed foule, that ftruggling to be free,
Art more ingaged; helpe Angels make affay,
Bowe ftubborne knees, and hart with ftrings of fteal,
Be foft as finnewes of the new borne babe,
All may be well.

Now Prince Hamlet was half down the stairs, a foot of
sword-blade flashing under his hand.

Trembling and with all his muscles tense, his eyes
flashing like the steel, yet recoiling from the act, mutter-
ing.

Saying to himself and to his audience:

Now might I doe it, pat now a is praying,
And now Ile doo't, and fo a goes to heauen,
And fo am I reuendge, that would be fcand:
A villaine kills my father, and for that,
I his fole fonne, doe this fame villaine fend
To heauen.
Why, this is hire and falary, not reuendge,
A tooke my father grofly full of bread,
Withall his crimes braod blowne, as flufh as May,
And how his audit ftands who knows faue heauen,
But in our circumftance and courfe of thought,
Tis heauy with him: and am I then reuendged
To take him in the purging of his foule,
When he is fit and feafond for his paffage?
No.
Vp fword, and knowe thou a more horrid hent,
When he is drunke, a fleepe, or in his rage,
Or in th'inceftious pleafure of his bed,
At game a fwearing, or about fome act
That has no relifh of faluation in't,
Then trip him that his heels may kick at heauen,
And that his foule may be as damnd and black
As hell wherto it goes; my mother ftaies,
This phifick but prolongs thy fickly daies.

And he was off to flay his mother with words, quivering
with anger and self-contempt, knowing his weakness.
King Claudius was rising from the faldstool, ignorant of
the danger that had passed by him.

My words fly vp, my thoughts remaine belowe,
Words without thoughts neuer to heuen goe.

A rhyming couplet, neat and compelling as the audience's
sigh of relief. And the curtain was coming weightily
down.

Even when I had first read this play at school, and before it had any private meaning for me, I pitied King Claudius in this scene and hated Prince Hamlet for his decision. If the king was to die, let him die now in at least the effort of prayer. To wait until King Claudius was bestial and despatch him then—the filthiest wickedness of deliberation and the calculating mind and lack of all sense of human worth, for even the king was a man.

When I was slain and while I was still in rebellion against my death I thought of the gods as a kind of Prince Hamlet who had carefully planned the day and the hour, and I made all this the symbol for a great deal of private suffering and revulsion. I was deprived of sight at a time when my eyes were labouring in bestiality and altogether unprepared. I was adolescent. The life of my eyes had become one of continual erotic curiosity. They had not grown up, but existed for the purpose of drawing out of all that they saw material for the low fires, the smouldering fantasy of my brain.

I was nearly twenty-three. In many ways I was mature. My work satisfied me, and they said I should be a good surgeon, possibly a great one, for I was musical too and had a musician's hands, and that kind of touch very rarely goes with a surgeon's touch, the caressive with the incisive, but tends to be confined to people whose lives are otherwise directed by the abstract mind—natural mathematicians. I promised well and I worked well. I neglected nothing, as I thought. I went about and met people. I was a swimmer, and I ran. I dressed with care and adjusted my politics, my tastes and my manners.

And when the pains came on again I behaved if any-thing only too reasonably and well.

Whether I had any foreknowledge I do not know. My life had flow and direction. I wanted to get on with whatever came next, and I refused to think about myself until it was all over.

Almost before there was any inflammation I put my-self into the hands of the only neurologist visiting the hospital I worked in. It was, in fact, too early for a com-plete diagnosis. I had pains in the head, and that was all. A continual headache which made work difficult, very little more. To-day I fancy they would have got me ear-lier, but this was just after the Great War, and I had to wait for several weeks and insist on continual examina-tion before all of a sudden they woke up.

They said:

'Glioma . . . Cut. . . .'

I gritted my teeth and refused to think, and said:

'Right. Get on with it.'

And that was that—until I came round. I have no memory of hospital scenes and no recollection of any but other people's anxieties and panics. When my parents and my brother came I took a firm line with them and was impatient—almost as if they were trying to stop me doing something that I very much wanted to do.

I am not sure now whether to be glad or otherwise about the way I took it. I think it was a kind of spiritual madness. I also think it had a good deal of essential cowardice in it, like the spectacular self-violations that Japanese noblemen hypnotise themselves into. I refused to think, and that is always bad. And I am inclined to feel that I ought to have allowed myself to panic before the operation took place. Panic is a kind of possible safety-valve and, more than that—a possible means of purgation. It is bad when it is indulged. It is just as bad, I suspect, when it is inhibited. I should have thought hard and allowed myself all the feelings appropriate to the situation. I didn't. I clenched myself hard. I was lying to myself, pretending that it was a matter of pain to be undergone blandly for the sake of a good end—immolation for the cause, Flora Macdonald or whoever it was with her arm barring the door. And the result was that I lost an opportunity of making my peace with the objects of sight. It was a rebellious and ungraceful death-bed.

On the other hand, I escaped fear, more or less. And I have seen terrible effects wrought by fear in the minds of a great many kinds of people.

But I escaped fear only to fall, when it was all over, into despair.

I had not tamed my eyes before they left me. It was a fatal weakness, I thought now. In those parts of me which were catered for by the senses I still had with me I was fairly mature. My vision had remained adolescent. I had still been able to be sexually excited by things merely seen—by nakedness, for instance, and by the innumerable images of it. I only now began to realise this. The visual images that my mind retained were nearly all of a definitely erotic flavour. I should have prepared myself by contemplating those things which are calm and durable. I should have spent my last few days of sight in looking at the trees and the street and the people in the street out of my window and have asked my friends to bring me reproductions of fine, tranquil pictures. Instead I had let my eyes rest on a very attractive nurse and follow her movements with intricate fascination. I had been vaguely titillated by the visible presence of the one or two young women who were brought along by my friends when they came to see me.

And of these were the images that were dominant in my mind when I returned to life after the operation. When the attractive nurse came to my bedside I was unable to receive the impact of her presence in my remaining senses. I remembered how she had looked—and desperately wanted to look again.

My eyes had been alive with youthful itch when I parted with them. I very quickly realised it. And I thought that I should remain to the end of my life thus locked, clogged, with a head full of the erotic images of adolescence, and in consequence never become truly mature at all, at least in my relations with women. It terrified me. In a very short time I had become self-conscious. I already had a certain amount of what is called experience, and I had felt good about it at the time, but it had been considerably less than adult as I now understood. I wanted to open my eyes for a year, a month, a week, and make the effort to see life steadily and see it whole, and then I would be content to close them again for good. I was frightened. I thought of nothing else for several weeks, and it delayed my recovery not a little.

I saw myself as one caught in an obscene gesture and frozen, petrified in that gesture to eternity.

> When he is drunke, a fleepe, or in his rage,
> Or in th'inceftious pleafure of his bed,
> At game a fwearing, or about fome act
> That has no relifh of faluation in't,
> Then trip him that his heels may kick at heauen,
> And that his foule may be as damnd and black....

I was not ready. And I was in for a very bad time when I tried seriously to adjust myself to the new life.

> If thine eye offend thee, pluck it out, and cast it from thee...

Ah, no. For the eye is not a thing existing unto itself. It is a channel through which the whole creature is living. If the eye offends, that is the moment at which it should least of all be plucked out. Wait. Let the channel purify itself and new, fresh waters pour in to purify all the connected channels within. *If thine eye offend thee* . . . then art thou offence from top to toe and filled with the rankness poured into thee by way of thine eye. . . . And to pluck out the eye then is to seal up the offence in a man.

I need not have worried. In a world composed largely of adolescent people I was homoepathically cured by the adolescence of women I met. And it did not take very long.

But six months of the new life were a nightmare. I rebelled. I would not concentrate on learning, on the massive task of reducing all things formerly seen to objects of touch, of touch, smell and hearing, on reading with the tips of my fingers and trusting my movements to a natural sense of balance and trusting other people not to mislead me, not realising yet how the faculties withdraw to a centre, however diminished, and concentrate themselves afresh in such a way that I have often felt myself to be more and not less powerful for lacking one of the instruments of power.

I rebelled. I was like a man on his first solitary voyage abroad, who knows the foreign language and uses it when necessary, but who will not learn to think in the foreign language and so remains unliberated in mind, closed up in the darkness of his own thoughts and pinned to his native shore, oppressed by the bridges that he refuses to burn.

And my dreams were bad. I awoke almost every morning with the same fantasy in my head. I was coming out of a dream in which I was prevented from opening my eyes and must struggle to awake in the knowledge that then I could open them and see where I was and how the easy, familiar world around me fared. And then I lay awake, concentrating myself on the moment when I should lift my lids, fancying myself aware of the colours of the morning sun that lay warm upon them. And as I lay and slowly understood that the dream was real and the awakening a mirage a light sweat broke out and the beads of it lay on my eyelids, and I turned and groaned and prayed to sleep again.

I was tortured by memory. I could still conjure my visual images, and that was my torture. Glioma. . . . The disease should have destroyed all the inner channels of sight too. Or else the delicate edge of the knife should have drawn out with my eyes unnecessary nerve and left me free not to remember. I cannot remember the moment at which I ceased to rebel. I suppose the transformation went on underneath all the time and that rebellion was only the superficial shedding of dead leaves.

But I could not go straight on with my work, not even with the new twist that eyelessness imposed on it. I had to learn to walk all over again. And I was carried back into the deep places of my childhood in the attempt to find a principle of continuity between the old life and the new. I found none. I went home, and I found nothing but a principle of mortification. The life there, now that I could perceive it without prejudice, I saw to be a life of inventing work to do in order that there might be work to be done. I sat in the garden and heard my mother wearing herself out superintending the daily help and driving her on to ever greater orgies of unnecessary cleaning. It was a life that stood still in the after-dinner noises of washing-up. I developed a permanent horror of kitchens and persuaded my father to give me the money to go back to London at once and begin my osteopathy and massage now while I was still largely helpless.

When other people have talked to me about their childhood and their family background I have always found that they derived most satisfaction from the anecdotes they were able to tell of their immediate relatives. The families in which curious little incidents abound are the families which provide their children with a rich

60

and satisfying background. Distinguished, learned and wealthy fathers give their children very little. Eccentric fathers often sow in them the seeds of greatness. To belong to a family in which a great deal happens is the important thing, or to be continually disturbed by wayward and unaccountable humours. These if they do nothing else at any rate prohibit the growth of that overwhelming consciousness of the fixed rightness of the mature adult which is so stifling an influence on the spontaneity of most of the people one meets. Their emptiness flourishes to the end of their lives. And it is in this sense that I feel that my own family background and my own childhood experience were impoverished. Norwich is a beautiful city, and a great deal happens there. My father was a good man and well-to-do. We had many relatives and family friends. But a blight of decorum and monotonously consistent behaviour left the whole of that life dead and unburgeoning for me. My life began only when I got away from home. I had to exert my imagination more than a man should if he is to remain a free and spontaneous being. And I remember no more than two anecdotes current in the family which I was ever able to call on as being worth the telling or as giving any quality of depth, reality and excitement to the first sixteen years of my life.

My brother fought in the Great War. I was too young. I do not think my brother would have gone of his own choice. He was a teetotaller and not very friendly. And as a schoolmaster he could have stayed at home. But the people of Norwich regarded us with suspicion and on several occasions ventilated a belief that we were German spies. Our name is German. My father, although a J.P. and one greatly respected by his associates, was a big, heavy man with the sort of cropped head which the newspaper cartoons were beginning to make familiar. And he had in fact been born in Amsterdam, which was as near Germany as made no difference—to the people of Norwich. So he decided that Arthur had better go. Arthur went. He saw undistinguished service on the Western Front and came home in 1919 quite unharmed. Except in one respect . . . Arthur had the same head of thick and naturally wavy hair as our mother and myself, and he was a little vain. He had sufficient strength of character to care nothing at all for the opinion of his fellow soldiers, who were mostly yokels, and when he discovered that the Army administered a potion of rum to its sons at moments of crisis he accepted his share, although as I say he was a teetotaller. It was difficult for Arthur to get hold of any good brilliantine or other dressing in France, and he had the impression that rum was good for the hair, doubtless associating it with a dressing he had previously heard of called Bay Rum, which is something quite different. And so, when the rations of rum came round, Arthur always took his ration, disregarding the snarls and ribaldry of his companions, and at once poured it over his hair and rubbed it into the scalp. The result was that when he came home in 1919 his luxurious hair had begun to fall and that in a few months his head was as bald as an egg.

So far as I can see this tale has no moral. Our mother

used to think it had and often told it as a discouragement to young people who, in her opinion, took too much pride in their appearance. But in fact it is pure anecdote with the gratuitous disinterestedness of all great works of art. The other family tale that I remember is, on the contrary, all moral. It concerns Aunt Elizabeth's egg-timer. There were no advanced ideas in our family, and our Aunt Elizabeth, who lived on a farm about twelve miles out of Norwich, was, if anything, more backward than the rest of us. But when her husband died she quite unexpectedly took it into her head to have him cremated and after the cremation took his ashes to a hardware store and had them made into an egg-timer. When my mother ventured to express a doubt as to the propriety of such an act our Aunt Elizabeth said that her husband had been no use while he was alive, and so she meant to put him to some use now. And that was all. As a boy I accepted my family's attitude to Aunt Elizabeth's egg-timer. It was a mixed attitude of outrage at the sacrilege and secret pride in the eccentricity. But many years later I remembered Aunt Elizabeth's egg-timer as the one truly poetic thing which the monotonous life of our family had cast up in its time. And not many years ago, when all the rest of the family had been a good while dead, I made a pilgrimage to Aunt Elizabeth at her farm, especially, I believe, to handle the egg-timer. I pictured myself holding it between my finger tips and feeling the slight vibration of the glass as the ashes trickled through, and considering with a profound emotion that here I held all the residues of the life of a man, an ashen soul flowing between the tips of my fingers. But I have never been into any room that so oppressed me with its drabness as did Aunt Elizabeth's kitchen on that day. Aunt Elizabeth herself was a querulous old woman now, but in only too complete possession of her more commonplace faculties. And she did not remember the egg-timer at first, and even when I brought it to her mind, could not think why on earth I should be interested in it. She used a stop-watch now, and that she thought was much more interesting. I did not press the point. I was filled with an awful sense of desolation. And I knew that if Aunt Elizabeth went rooting about on her shelves and got me the egg-timer it would feel no different from those that cost a shilling at any store—and that it would be no different. Ashes were ashes, and sand was sand. And the sea-shore and the sand-pits no doubt hold mysteries greater than Aunt Elizabeth over elicited from a dead husband who had been no use to her when he was alive.

But in the streets about my home I remember blind men. And I remember how I pitied them and how I turned away and would not look at them or think about them because I did not like the feeling of pity. I remember one whom I used to meet almost every morning on my way to school, and how one morning I bumped against him while I was looking across the road and did not hear his stick tapping along the pavement, and how faint I turned at the sight of his face smiling patiently beneath the dark glasses, and how soft and gentle like a woman's his voice was. There was also a piano-tuner who came to the house, but although I was the only one in the house who played the piano I always managed to be out of the way when he called and never saw him except once through the frosted glass of the door. I became hardened as I grew older, and the blind beggar at the market with the terrier sitting beside him and the three men I saw in hospital blue towards the end of the war, and those I saw later tapping with their sticks along the London pavements or helped off buses by grave-faced conductors, and across the road by iittle, tight-lipped women in pince-nez, affected me hardly at all. I have conjured up their images since and recalled my feelings towards them at the time, and have felt more in need of prayers for the world at those moments than on any other occasion.

For this and for a variety of other reasons I feel that I have the right and the obligation to myself of demanding and receiving more in physical love than another person. For love is touch, and I am touch. My only profound contact with any other person is tactile. Woman I know only as a lover or as a patient, and very frequently indeed the latter will demand to be the former as the natural completion of a process.

I do not feel that I exceed my rights. I have sometimes felt that I fail in my obligations. They are very narrow in scope. The world I live in is small.

One of my dearest pleasures between the ages of fourteen and twenty lay in turning over the pages of an atlas. I was particularly fond of population maps and those showing the distribution of races and occupations. I could build up from these a world swarming with miniature people who went about their ways regardless of the giant eye which observed them from above as through a microscope. I was the god of this world, and even when I left my atlas behind and walked out in the streets or on a hillside it was with a map-maker's vision that I saw the world around me. I would derive great satisfaction from such thoughts as that neither Australia nor yet New Zealand was the antipodes of the ground I stood on, as is often supposed, but only a waste of waters. New Zealand I knew lay counter to Spain. And the antipodes to all this land we look upon as our world, from the south of France to the north of Scandinavia, was nothing at all, a wilderness, a waste, latitudes peopled only by the wind. Now my world has drawn in. It is smaller than the world of an unimaginative man. And its weight is sometimes intolerable. The only thing that gives me any sensation of distance is to hear a sound reaching me across a valley or on the open sea. Echoes only tell me of the masses of height against which they ring. I am Atlas. Formerly I was a god who contemplated all things airily from above. Now I bear the world upon my own shoulders as a burden which I cannot so much as turn to see. The light is all above my head. I live in darkness. The world is mass, anguish of the weight, sultry weather and incomprehension. I am glad. It is nearer to religious truth. And it also makes possible that moment when the burden is eased, although the darkness remains. Men have pitied Atlas. They have not realised that at some time late in his life, whether out of mercy or pure diversion, the chief of the gods must have exulted to lift the world for a moment and give the bowed creature's shoulders a space in which to free themselves painfully of cramp and then to experience the delight of their own unlimited strength in a weightless void. The years that followed can have meant nothing to an Atlas living with that moment exquisitely treasured in his mind.

CHAPTER FOUR

By six o'clock the occasional chugging of a bird's throat had grown up into a strenuous, busy clamour at my window. On my window-sill the multitude of tiny spears that were jasmine leaves rustled together. And presently, as of a ghostly visitor, I was aware of light in the room and the invasion of morning sun that increased upon my face.

I fancy that it must have been Sunday that day. It has a Sunday feeling in the memory.

There must have been church bells in the evening and the yawning sense of interruption and of people trying desperately hard to be lazy to-day because the Bible enjoined it, and filling in the time by putting on their best clothes and solemnest moods and going for walks and talking in groups at the chapel gates. I hate Sunday for its hushed voices, whispering scandal on the way home from a service. It is the day of freedom and the day on which English people demonstrate that they have not yet learnt what to do with freedom, but can only herd themselves into places of worship and public parks and eat the same food as every one of their neighbours and tell each other all the stories which they would be too charitable to repeat on any other day of the week. I hate Sunday, in fact, because it is the one day in the week which bears not the slightest mark of any religious feeling.

But I may have my dates wrong, and I may be remembering this third day at Rose Gwavas as a Sunday only because it was a hateful day. And so for that matter were the two or three days that followed it. I remember them vaguely as days of waiting for something, aimless, suspended days.

The house was hollow, and I was hollow. Tedium reigned.

I remember that the weather was a little oppressive, despite the sun, as though a storm were passing us two or three miles to the south. I remember John Madron going about the house and being attentive to his aunt and to me, his footsteps like donkeys' hooves on the naked boards or deadened in thick carpets, and the wooden latches of the doors lifting and dropping neatly into place. And I remember that I turned my attention at last to the new Bechstein which Mrs. Nance had installed in a room too heavily curtained for my ear and holding nothing else but a couple of Louis XIV chairs and an ash-tray.

I played, I suppose, what I do play when the mood is not what it might be—things heard and only half remembered, a prolonged improvisation upon everything and nothing. I must have done it with conviction because I remember that Mrs. Nance came into the room and sat down and listened to me for as much as an hour at a time.

I lost and found myself in the music and lost myself again. At one moment I would be under water in the tides of sound, myself their agent and my fingers ten small instruments played against their will or mine. At another moment I would come to the surface and be outside the music altogether and considering the movements of my fingers with detached amusement. Then I would discover that Mrs. Nance was in the room, and I would exchange remarks with her as I played and then suddenly wish that she were not there and plunge down into the ocean of sounds again to escape her, and remain hidden in its depths until she went away or until forgot her.

And so it went on. As I remember it I can imagine now that I played without stopping for three or four days on end and that it was a curious, spiritual Marathon contrived for the purpose of evading thought and feeling, playing amorously with the tedium until Sophie came back.

For during those few, aimless days Sophie Madron did not put in an appearance at all. Nobody at Rose Gwavas mentioned her absence, but it may have been what infected everybody there with whatever it was they were infected with.

I was sitting out on the lawn when Sophie came back. It was just before lunch, and the sun was brilliant and dry. I sat in a deck-chair fingering *Thus Spake Zarathustra,* and amusing myself with the German barbarian's approach to French civilisation as represented here in Friedrich Nietzsche's pathetic attempt to prefer the music of Offenbach to his countryman Richard Wagner's massive organisation of guttural noises. There was a sudden scattering of gravel, and Sophie Madron was stepping high-heeled and a little defiant towards the house.

'Good morning,' she said.

She said it in a voice made as off-hand as possible, but not without its note of self-consciousness and tension.

It was as if she said:

'Don't you dare wonder where I've been, my good man.'

I probably smiled as I returned her greeting, and my smile probably annoyed her. At any rate, she went straight into the house without another word, and I put *Thus Spake Zarathustra* down on the grass and stretched and yawned and presently got up and walked round the lawn, touching the bushy feathers of spiræa and carefully removing all traces of smile from my face before I went in presently to lunch.

We went into the village. Betty des Voeux had come round to tea and wanted to do some shopping afterwards. So did Sophie. Mrs. Nance suggested that I also went. John drove us in.

Everybody was silent except Betty des Voeux. John was in a bad temper. I suppose he was angry with Sophie. He and Mrs. Nance had shown a tendency already at lunch to argue about apparently harmless topics like the weather, and I fancied that it was really a clash about Sophie, who had sat withdrawn into herself and nursing something of her own. It was the same as we drove into Gwavas after tea except that Mrs. Nance was not there for John to fight with.

When we started home again Betty des Voeux suggested a drink at the Gilded Lamb. The Gilded Lamb was in Pentreath. We followed the sea-front round the Pentreath pier-head and the fish-market and up on the cliff towards the quarries end.

At the Gilded Lamb we found the young man who had been at Rose Gwavas on the morning after my arrival. There was a girl with him whose name was Jill. The young man's name was Trevor Beed, and I recall very little else of him but his voice, at once metallic and plangent like a banjo string. I imagined him to have a closely trimmed moustache, but I never remembered to ask about it. His Jill was a background person, evidently attractive enough to please Mr. Beed, but unobtrusive and quite without Betty des Voeux's vitality, though no doubt similarly blonde and living by the same values.

Betty des Voeux and Jill drank gin. Trevor Beed and John drank sixpenny ale in pints. Sophie and I drank fivepenny beer in half pints.

We presently found ourselves leaving the Gilded Lamb to drive out beyond the quarries to Four Tides. Six people crowded into John's car. Jill sat on Trevor Beed's knee in the back. I was sitting in the back. Sophie manœuvred Betty des Voeux into the back to sit on my knee.

Betty des Voeux sat stiffly at first with one hand on John's shoulder in front, but finding that I seemed to be a man like any other, gradually assumed a more comfortable position and reclined against me, warm and heavy, a healthy, mature and unequivocally attractive female. Her sitting thus and also perhaps the fact that it was Sophie who had manœuvred her into it appeared to incense John further, for he put his foot down on the accelerator and drove recklessly fast along the winding coast road until we pulled up before the Sloop Inn at Four Tides.

Four Tides, I had already gathered, was a rather self-conscious village. It was, perhaps, too picturesque, and attracted not only artists but also well-to-do people of less aggressively æsthetic bias. The local fishermen had wisely taken advantage of these additions to the population. The decline of inshore fishing is one of the saddest features of contemporary English life, and the Four Tides fishermen had been only too glad to earn money by sitting to a painter or being the life and soul of a highbrow party or becoming the temporary paramour of some widow with a taste for the recherché in men. Every fisherman in the village was a character and knew it, and prospered according to his talent.

The Sloop Inn was the only pub in Four Tides and the main focus of this curiously vicious village life, with the possible exception of a row of three cottages across the way which a Mrs. Allison, one-time toast of Ebury Street and Montparnasse, had turned into a mixture of chintz tea shoppë and private hotel called the Scallop Shell. Mrs. Allison was reputed to be a superlatively charming, highly gifted woman, but I did not meet her, though I have friends who also knew her in London.

I did not, in fact, penetrate the Bohemia of Four Tides at all. I had it analysed for me in various tones of voice by different people, and on this particular evening I heard through a noise of tankards and furniture the voices of some of the Bohemians.

The corner immediately opposite me contained an American voice. Or rather it contained a New England accent. The voice sustaining the accent was a thin, wet voice of no nationality in particular. This voice talked about Picasso, Dali and Kandinsky to some of a group of excitable voices with variously diluted Oxford accents who seemed on the whole, however, to be more concerned with some private form of ribaldry than with contemporary art, and who, I fancy, regarded us in the opposite corner with a certain amount of hostility and contempt. Our social alliances were rather with the smaller groups to the right and left of us. To the right by the fireplace were two young men whose Oxford accents were not in the least diluted, and who I fancied had small moustaches, like Trevor Beed, and very red faces. They also had pipes in their mouths, which accentuated the manliness and monosyllabic tempo of their conversation. They were talking with a fisherman about a shark he professed to have caught and arranging a trip out with him for the following night, and recalling to each other previous hunting, shooting and fishing exploits of their own, which made them laugh in a throaty, manly and reserved way. On our left were three people who had to be explained to me. They spoke very little. Betty des Voeux whispered to me that the girl in the middle was a very attractive, sulky little piece, that the man on this side of her was her husband, and that on the other side of her sat the cox'n of the Gwavas lifeboat, a handsome, middle-aged fisherman, whom all the ladies of Four Tides pursued and whom the husband of this girl rightly suspected of being his wife's occasional lover.

Other people came in during the course of the evening, including a married couple whom nobody seemed to like very much, because the wife was Lesbian and the husband homosexual, and their marriage a convenient framework within which each of them could seduce the other's unsuspecting friends. Others, too, all of whom enjoyed some distinction or other. But it was too early in the year for the floating population of Four Tides to have fully assembled.

Our conversation slowly closed in upon itself. The girl called Jill, who had hitherto had nothing to say, introduced the topic of the new building scheme and the demolition of cottages.

It was an old topic. The fight was over. Protest had been made to the Minister of Health. A deputation of nine fishermen had sailed up to London in a tiny drifter, and the Minister of Health had received them kindly. It had been dramatically done. As the tiny drifter bobbed up and down on a grey, November tide, all the women of Four Tides and Pentreath had gathered on Pentreath north jetty, singing 'Fight the Good Fight . . .' and a single ray of sun had fallen upon the boat and followed it out to sea. The newspapers had made a story of it. It was a battle between fishermen and the builders on the town council, for the fishermen would have nowhere to dry their nets, and they would have to climb the steep hill to and from their new homes, but the artists and the local gentry had made common cause with them because the old, condemned cottages are picturesque. Now it was all over. The building scheme was under way. Some of the people had already moved up the hill to their new, flimsy houses and were very pleased indeed with them. It was nice to have a bit of garden and a view. The only people still interested were the artists and the local gentry who felt that the place was losing its traditional charm and becoming vulgarised, and that the builders on the council had won a victory over them.

Jill had heard that an epidemic of scarlet fever had already broken out in the new houses, and that pleased everybody very much. They revived their antagonism and railed at the building trade.

I suggested that perhaps the Government wanted to clear away the narrow, winding roads in order to have a clear route to Land's End for purposes of national defence.

That stopped the conversation for a moment. They were quite ready to characterize the local building trade as full of damned Reds, but this could hardly be thought to apply to the Government at that time. And there was an airport at Land's End, and the Scillies were a very likely naval base.

It was Sophie who pointed out these last two facts. I was aware of her rousing herself at my comment and seeking a political alliance with me against the others. That wasn't a kind of alliance I wanted, so I closed down.

During the pause we had a new round of drinks, for which I made it my turn to pay. After the first sip Mr. Beed turned to me sympathetically again and made as if trying to enlist me on their side and at the same time make a point of reconciliation all round.

'Well, anyway,' he said, 'there is one thing about this

building scheme. It'll keep the tourist population down. There won't be so many visitors when the old villages are gone.'

But Sophie wouldn't subside.

'I can't think why you dislike the visitors so much,' she said. 'You both admire the same things.'

And that was true enough. It was picturesque charm which attracted the tourist population, and it was precisely this which Trevor Beed and Jill, Betty des Voeux and John and all their local friends were so anxious to conserve. It was a world of Cornish cream and khaki shorts for them too.

Again there was a pause. It was broken this time by John Madron, who had some views to urge on the general condition of the world. They were very similar to those urged in the writing of Lord Beaverbrook, and not unlike the main drift of a pamphlet by Sir Oswald Mosley, which somebody had read to me. It was largely a question of democracy having failed because it exalted the industrial workers at the expense of agriculture and the country-side.

Sophie was sitting tense and silent somewhere to the right of me. I would not argue, but I kept wanting to prompt her with the correct things to say. Not because I thought them of any importance, but because I wanted Sophie to be free of her anger and tension. It was no more natural to her than the schoolgirl enthusiasm of the other day. I wanted her to be free to withdraw into herself again and deal with the real hurt, whatever it was, that she was nursing. But every moment the conversation became more distasteful to me, and the more distasteful it became the more she was involved in it, and at the same time the more speechless, tense and frustrated she was.

We drifted over foreign peoples. Trevor Beed and John were full of admiration for the Germans. I was a little puzzled at first. To their fathers all foreigners had been the same, and this looked at first like a highly admirable development in international tolerance. Alas, no. Trevor Beed recounted some personal encounters with individual Germans and individual Frenchmen, and it became obvious that his preference for the Germans depended entirely on the fact that they were hardly distinguishable from Englishmen in the most important respects, and that his admiration for the Germans was in fact only a projected hatred of the French and all other races of dark, excitable nature. He certainly hated the French most of all. The Italians he thought were at last beginning to pull themselves together and behave as if they were not a Latin race at all. And it looked as if Spain too. . . . I suggested that all the Latin races and especially the French had still a thing or two they might teach us about leading the civilised life. It seemed that I could not altogether escape aligning myself politically with Sophie, for she agreed with me in tones which were those of gratitude. But it was precisely this French talent for living which outraged Mr. Beed most of all. The French were not only lazy, dirty and dishonest, like the Breton ond Ostend fishermen who frequented Pentreath harbour and whom the local Cornish fishermen showed their soundness of mind by lumping together as 'dirty Belgiques,' but they were even at their best cynical, degenerate sensualists whose attitude to women in particular . . . I perceived his drift. Mr. Beed looked round, I am sure, at the group in the opposite corner and fetched up from a great depth the remark he had been wanting to make all the evening.

'I think we ought to have conscription in this country,' he said. 'It would do everybody good.'

There was no limit to Sophie's anger. She began to say something and then stopped, and I was aware of her trembling with such a pressure of feeling that I fancied she might faint with it or get up and sweep all the glasses off the table and stamp out.

I wanted to prompt her with what to say:

'Don't you try to conscript me, little man.'

I wanted to tell her to void her anger and unhinge Mr. Beed with some little insult like that, and then to take her hand and explain to her carefully just why Mr. Beed both hated the French and demanded conscription alike for himself and for the people he disapproved of in this country.

But as a matter of fact she knew.

Betty des Voeux and Jill had dropped out of the conversation. It was a conversation between men, and the awful thing was that it had become a terribly sincere, meaningful conversation. If someone had played X-rays upon John Madron and Trevor Beed at that moment he would have seen the emotions of chivalry and an awful craving for duty jetting up in their breast like coloured fluids in the glass tubes of a siphon system.

John gave expression to the mood by suddenly getting up and announcing that he'd better go and ring Auntie up and tell her they'd be rather late in.

Sophie giggled.

John went out of the room, and there was a moment's pause. Then Sophie said, 'Trevor, darling,' in a languishing voice, and there was a piece of dumb-play which I had no means of perceiving, followed by a doubtful snicker from Betty des Voeux and an embarrassed silence which lasted until John came back and said that Mrs. Nance was going to bed and suggested that we had some bread and cheese here at the pub before driving on.

A few minutes after ten John wondered if they should go now. He'd have to drive Trevor Beed and Jill home, and it might be best to make that a separate trip and get back before closing time to pick up Sophie and me.

I was left alone with Sophie. Betty des Voeux wanted to stay behind till John came back, but John disagreed.

Sophie was thoroughly unhappy now. Anger and the desire to taunt had both subsided. She lit a cigarette, and I was aware of her leaning forward with her elbows and propping her weight on the table. Then it was as if she found the position too aggressive, too self-assured for her mood. She played about in the ash-tray with her cigarette and finally left it there to burn acridly away and sat back in her corner with, I should think, her hands a little awkwardly in her lap.

'The men are all alike round here,' she said. 'They're all crucified.'

I let it sink in. I thought I knew what she meant.

'Yes, I suppose they are. But tell me,' I said. 'I didn't quite follow the conversation to the end. Somebody . . .'

Sophie laughed.

'That was it. You mean when I touched Trevor's face? I thought I'd fondle his cheek and see what the response was.'

'And what was it?'

'Oh, he stood to attention. You know . . .'

'Yes. Do I?'

'I think so.'

And we sat in silence.

Sophie seemed to be watching the people in the opposite corner.

Presently she said:

'Those people over there are crucified too, I suppose. But they do know it. I think there's quite a lot to be said for living in despair.'

'Yes . . .?'

'It means you only kid yourself from moment to moment, at any rate.'

And that was all I got for the moment.

I puzzled over Sophie's mood. I think I was looking for something too subtle in it. Or perhaps I only understood neurotic women at that time. At any rate, when the simple thing overtook me, I was not altogether prepared for it.

We decided to go before closing time and trust to meeting John on the road. The tide was ebbing, and as we stepped outside the door of the Sloop Inn the agreeable pungency of the harbour slime and the iodine of drying bladder-wrack assailed our nostrils, and there were late seagulls and jackdaws wheeling around and crying and a few men crying to each other across the harbour. We turned inland up a very steep road.

Neither of us said anything. I did not know whether Sophie was concentrating on private worries or on her attitude towards me. All I knew of her was her lilting step and her deeper breathing as we climbed the hill. I had no stick. My ear followed her movements.

A car came grinding heavily down the hill. I had to move quickly to the roadside and was glad to find myself standing on soft grass without having made any clumsy, stumbling or anxious movement. I had to stand there a moment until my ear found Sophie's movement again. A stream was making its way uncertainly down along the ditch towards the sea below.

As I rejoined Sophie on the road she said:

'We're on the wrong road. This isn't the way John will be coming.'

She said it in a tone of annoyance, but with a fundamental matter-of-factness which made me suspect that she might be testing my reactions.

I said:

'That's a pity.'

I said it with complete indifference, and I think that pleased her. I was still puzzling. A moment later she halted, and I stood waiting for her.

She said:

'Are you crucified?'

Her voice was laboured, and the taunt in it was not altogether convincing. I fumbled for her meaning. She was very close to me. I got the dark, violet scent she used and even I fancied her warmth and the motion of her breathing.

'I don't think so,' I said. 'Or at any rate not very much. . . .'

But I think I was trembling a little. And when the tips of her fingers reached my face I did not stand to attention.

One hand only and then two hands together passed over my face and stirred the roots of my hair and slowly withdrew again. I heard the girl Sophie Madron sigh. It was one of those long, deliberate sighs with which people try to regain absolute control of themselves when emotion has caught them below the heart and made their breathing tremulous.

We stood for a moment thus facing each other and then walked on again in silence. It was not until we reached the last stile on Rose Gwavas heath that we kissed or in any way touched each other. And then it was a long, deliberate kiss of preparation, cold and watchful.

Part Two

CHAPTER FIVE

MATING IS BEST when it is conducted at freezing-point. I do not mean by this that people ought to make love only round about Christmas or that lovers will derive the highest satisfaction from each other only when they keep the temperature of their bodies low, though there is something in this too. To have the point of immediate contact as the point of greatest heat or, as it were, to manufacture great heat out of nothing is not altogether worthless as an ideal in practice. What I mean, however, when I say that mating is best conducted at freezing-point is that in love which is to be fully satisfying to those engaged in it the emotional temperature must be kept down as low as is humanly possible.

The emotions must be caught and, as it were, frozen beforehand as the dental nerve is frozen with cocaine before the extraction of a tooth.

Among the people aware of this truth and able to explain why it is so are poets, good actors, the saints, Frenchmen and the manufacturers of many kinds of excellent gas and electric refrigerators now on the market. Those most notably ignorant of it are English people of the lower middle classes, and especially those whose minds have been most heavily saturated with poetry and mysticism, continental thought and the art of the theatre.

Poetry is like ice-cream. A great deal of heat is needed in the making of it, but all this heat must be generated in the poetic faculties precisely in order that the poetry itself may be frozen out and left in isolation lest it melt and run.

The actor who is to move his audience deeply must himself remain unmoved. He must stand apart from the part he is playing and watch himself coldly and concern himself not with the tragedy but only like a surgeon with the exposed nerves of his audience. This is not to say that the actor must be a cold man. On the contrary. The good actor is a man of extraordinary depth of feeling, a man emotionally rich above the average. But his emotion must be tapped and himself disintoxicated beforehand at rehearsal. If the feeling is strong in his heart it will be correspondingly feeble in his hands and features, and if it is not drawn away from his heart and set beforehand tingling in his eyes and on his finger-tips an audience will find his performance unconvincing. It is once again the identical process of refrigeration.

And so it is with the saints. A journalist writing of the Beatific Vision would undoubtedly characterise it as 'a wonderful emotional experience.' But read the saints. Read St. John of the Cross. Intensity of feeling is all done with beforehand in the various phases of what is called the Dark Night of the Soul. The spirit is full of passion and anxiety. And then, little by little, the emotions are withdrawn and the faculties suspended, and the spirit is still and cold, waiting with not so much as a tremor for penetration by the Holy Spirit which enters 'with infinite gentleness wounding the soul in its innermost, most intimate deep places.' It is cold, cold and perfect, undisturbed.

So it is with the mating of lovers. The preparation is courtship, and the courtship is a poet ardently wooing the language of his own experience or a temperamental actor behind the scenes or a saint at his prayers all night, trembling and breaking into a sweat with the effort to rid himself of self and of the hot, emotional needs, or the heat drawn out by heat from an inner chamber where the water changes to ice.

'I come straight from the arms of another man,' she said. 'But I did have a bath.'

I was standing with my arms propped on the ledge and my head and shoulders buried or framed within the little alcove of her window. I had just opened the window. The air was chilly and scented. There was no creeper at this window, but it seemed to be above the cornice of the door I knew, and the light fragrance that came up to me must have been from the unbruised tips of the myrtles below or from leaves lightly bruised by tapping against the wall in the movement of the air.

'I did have a bath,' she said.

She was somewhere in the middle of the room. I couldn't tell exactly what she was doing. I heard no more than her breathing and the faint rustle of her clothes which, in any case, was lost in the stirring of the night outside.

A fox barked.

I turned away from the window and found my way to her dressing-table in the corner. It was a room almost completely empty of things. There were no books, no ornaments or pictures and no flowers. Cupboards on either side of the new, unused brick fireplace had been set plumb with the wall and the handles let into the wood. The dressing-table, which I came to now, was built low and plain in unvarnished wood of a very fine grain, a grain that I could not place, with a mirror let into the wall behind it and a glazed top that bore only two or three pots of cream and packets of tissues and not so much as a single brush.

But the brush was in Sophie's hand. She had just now begun to brush her hair. I listened to the deeply swishing music and learned from it now that Sophie's hair was short and also that it was very much alive, electrical, lifting up and clinging with its own life to the strokes of the brush in her hand.

The room did not feel bare. I could not imagine that Sophie lived in a bare room. Had I been able to see I should have found it bright with a wide, transparent pallor and great patches of sudden colour.

In any case the carpet was thick, very thick. I probed it with the toe of my shoe.

'It's a very lovely carpet,' she said. 'It hasn't any colour. It's just a sort of bright unbleachedness, pure oatmeal.'

'And the walls?'

'Dead lemon.'

'Where does the colour come in, then?'

'On the counterpane. Wide, wide circles of red and **yellow**.'

She had stopped brushing her hair. For a moment she

was quite still, and then she came very close to me and was putting her brush down on the dressing-table near to where my hand rested. She stood a moment, warm and sweet-smelling, near me and then returned to her place which I fancied was sitting on the edge of the bed.

I also stood quite still for a moment and then walked around the room again, remembering where the few palpable objects were and touching them. I crouched down by the fireplace, facing Sophie directly, so far as I knew, and with my finger-tips resting on the sharp edges of new brick and then on the deep pile of the carpet. I was a little troubled in mind by the strangeness of the room, this unfamiliar clarity, curiously virginal, which had become the natural abode of a person whom I deeply desired to know. It is terrifying to stand upon the brink of somebody else's life when there is nothing provided to deaden the senses into a decent acquiescence.

I thought I would stay here for a moment or two longer and then just go. I had forgotten all this while that Sophie Madron was not so much at peace with things as myself.

She said:

'You go nosing about my room like a little dog in a strange house.'

She said it in a little, laboured voice that told me plainly I was to come and sit beside her.

I crossed the room, and her fingers locked unsteadily in mine to guide me as I sat down on a very low bed. I put my hands to her shoulders and found that the silk of a dressing-gown slid smoothly upon fine, smooth skin under my fingers. It was unexpected. I had not realised

91

that she must have been undressing all this while and that now already she was expecting me to come to her as a lover.

I wanted to laugh. Then the desire to laugh had gone, and I was filled with terrible, sighing pity. That also passed, and I knew what to do.

I took my hands away from her shoulders. As I did so I felt the silk fall away and knew that except where it gathered itself again upon her folded hands and about her hips on the bed she was naked. She trembled and was then quite still. I put my hands upon her hands.

'Sophie Madron . . .' I said.

'Louis . . .'

'What do you want, Sophie Madron?'

She let her head drop forward upon my shoulder, and she was crying.

I said:

'If you don't fight now, you'll find yourself fighting me later.'

With her head fallen upon my shoulder she nodded, telling me that she knew.

Crying had already made her face hot. I could feel her breasts touching me lightly as if they were something in my pocket. I put the palms of my hands to her breasts, touching them from the side and from below, without moving her at all. Her breasts were clear and unmauled, fully ripe without any falling weight. I moved my hands to her sides and felt her body growing cooler as the heatedness of tears ebbed out of it.

'Shall I close the window?'

Her head rocked a little on my shoulder, saying no.

But I felt the tremor of coldness growing upon her skin and began to caress her to make the blood come tingling up to the surface again. At first she trembled, and her breathing became unsteady. Her lips were parted, and she turned from side to side, ready to moan. Then her mouth began to play bemusedly with my ear. The trembling ceased. Her breathing became steady. She lay upon her bed, quiet and wide-eyed, letting my fingers trace out her features. It was play now. I catalogued her features aloud as my fingers disengaged them and gathered up the single, mutable image of a deeply accented face and a body flowing perilously near to perfection from nape to heel and all the way home again, slender and fine, but capable of a sensuality in passion that might be frightening when it was fully awakened if its lover were inadequately ready. Her fingers rested limply in my neck and under my ear or followed the back of my hand as I explored her or wandered in my hair. And when I bent down at last to kiss her she lay with her cheek on the pillow like a child, promising to go to sleep at once. Only her mouth was scalding hot, being unassuaged.

For what are the emotions? They are things like anger, fear and curiosity. They are sudden changes in a man's temper, breaking in upon his existence and distorting his features. They are a man's immediate reaction to sudden, crude perceptions and while they are with him goad him into the helpless, obsessive performance of some crude and meaningless action like running away or striking another man in the face or peeping through a keyhole. It is true that civilised man very rarely suffers from emotion in a simple form. His emotions are mixed. More often than not his fear is diluted with anger and becomes a lingering resentment, just as his displays of anger are more often than not expressions of fear. He controls his features. Emotion operates at a slant in him, is oblique. His lust is impure. It is a compound of fear and curiosity as often as it is lust. Nevertheless these emotions remain with him, mixed as they are, and when a man is in their grip he is so much the less a man. The human impulses, those that arise in a man as such and have reference to the whole of his existence, are not emotions at all. Love is not an emotion. It is the whole of a man brought into play by a range of things perceived in which the elements of crude emotion are negligible. It is a new bias to the whole of his existence and a framework within which his emotions, when they operate, must learn to operate in a new way. Above all they must learn not to obtrude. A poem written in a state of emotional tension will be a fidgety, unfinished poem, and the colours will run. The sexual act, approached in a state of emotional tension will be premature, convulsive and unsatisfying to the point of nausea. It will be like the coupling of animals. For despite the point of view so heavily canvassed by contemporary writers like D. H. Lawrence, that we must become more animal, the simple fact of the matter is that animal love does not satisfy human beings even in their animal nature. It is not a question of despising one's animality. On the contrary. It is a question of realising that admirable as the animals may be in many ways they are inferior to human beings even in

94

their animality. Their sexual appetites are brief and suddenly exhausted as compared with the tenacity of human appetites, especially the appetites of the human female. Let us by all means admire and even worship the bull and the stallion as a symbol or as a god, but let us also understand that the bull's or the stallion's way of making love would not suffice us in the daily intercourse of our beds. A woman is more amorous, more ravenous in love than are all the beasts of the field and of the jungle together, and a man needs infinite cunning as well as his simple virility if he is not to leave her in some way raw and unsatisfied, though it is true that if he wishes to behave in an irresponsible manner a man can always keep a woman quiet for the time being by giving her a child. It is a counter development to the development of intelligence, bearing the intelligence down again to simple matters of sensation, man's equipoise, women forever appointed by some divine agency to see that man remains earth-bound and to prevent him from developing lopsidedly. Yet to make love in a state of emotional tension is, one gathers, a disease to which Englishmen of the middle classes and especially of the lower middle classes are notably prone. And the emotion which crops up to spoil things for them and for their unfortunate women friends seems to be in the majority of cases fear, in one of the many forms in which fear is so adept at concealing itself. Ignorance is, of course, the ubiquitous ally of emotion, of fear especially. And the hard-working, conscience-ridden schoolteacher or clerk, as a rule, has not even been told, not even informed, of the fact that he must make love coldly or that the lawyer in love is an edifying and not, as he has been taught to imagine, a disgraceful phenomenon. Extreme carefulness and detachment are the last things he associates with love. He thinks for instance that the best time to make love to a woman is when he is most inflamed with the desire to do so. He is even capable of supposing it a right and proper thing to go to a woman for consolation when he is feeling lonely and fretful. Alas, no. That ought to be possible. It would be very nice if something like the sexual act had been provided by the gods as a universal cure for mental sickness. But the brute fact is that man's pleasure in love is a derivative of the pleasure he gives to woman and that he cannot give pleasure to her in a fretful, disconsolate or in any way emotionally charged condition of mind. Love is one territory in which a genius for muddling through will not enable a man to muddle through.

The woman's need for quietude is a matter of greater consequence still. She must lie in the middle of wide, wide circles of peace, or she will suffer. There are some flowers that close up when you touch them, and there are some that open. A woman moves between the two. But there is a disease she may catch from men which makes her will to be open while nature bids her still be closed. And the disease is mortal. If it conquers her she lies full-blown and inert until the weather has finished with her. And that is the end. The conflict between nature and will is mortal in a woman. She must wait. There is a kind of certainty she knows as 'falling in love,' and she must wait on that. No matter how adept her lover she must have wide, wide circles of peace and in the middle of them herself lying in perfect watchfulness and certainty, or she will suffer.

But the sleeping mind is unaware of these things. In sleep the mind is governed by its anxieties and its greed. It is intoxicated. It cannot wait. It reaches out to possess and to coerce out of nothing a certainty. I awoke in a state of acute perturbation. The mind rejects in sleep its own prudent counsels of the night before. I fancied in sleep that I had already bound her to me and that now awakening I should find her sleeping happily beside me.

'Sophie. . . .'

I should put out a hand and find her warm and deeply breathing beside me. I should put my arms about her and kiss her an inch at a time into wakefulness. She would mutter and frown in sleep, and then at a given moment her eyes would open, and she would be awake and happily in bondage.

But I remembered. I had caressed her into momentary, partial quietude and then kissed her good night and left her. And at first I was terrified by the knowledge that she was still free and unbound to me.

Awakening is not the same thing for me as it is for other people. It is far more gradual. I lack the decisive moment at which one's eyes open and are flooded by the light of a world which had no existence but a few seconds ago. I came to life piecemeal. There was a lag and a division. The mind still in sleep, reaching back to adolescence and its own animal past, began to quarrel with the waking mind.

'You have lost a chance,' it said. 'Last night she turned

to you in a mood of exasperation and to-day will turn away again. You seem to forget the blue-eyed boy with whom she may be still in love.'

'Nicky Polgigga. . . .'

'Last night you could by your superior accomplishment in love have brought her away from him. This morning it will be too late. Already she has recoiled from you.'

'Under no circumstances,' said the waking mind, 'will I coerce love.'

'You will let her go?'

'If necessary.'

'You want her, don't you?'

'I do.'

'Then . . .?'

'It is she I want and not the bad half of a tricked woman.'

'You cannot sit still and expect the gods to pour out golden apples into your lap.'

'It is the only way to receive golden apples.'

'Fool, fool. A man is active and keen. He will not wait. Go to her now. . . .'

'Yes . . .?'

'. . . And at least know where you are. Ask her. Find out about Nicky Polgigga. Don't lay up trouble for yourself by planning without knowledge of the facts.'

'Does she know the facts?'

'Find out. Ask her what Nicky Polgigga means, what he is.'

'I have long made it a point of honour never to ask questions about herself of a woman in love.'

'You were taken off your guard last night. . . .'

'In a manner of speaking, yes.'

'You will admit that Miss Madron's behaviour was extraordinary, that it is unlikely to be repeated. . . .'

'It is for her to admit things about her own behaviour. I do not know her mind. I think there was an element of exasperation in her behaviour. I think she turned to me rather suddenly, even a little hysterically. Nevertheless . . .'

'Nevertheless . . .?'

'I think her instincts are fundamentally sound. And in any case. . . .'

The waking mind roused itself fully and raised its voice a little.

'. . . In any case,' it said, 'I shall have reserved to myself the melancholy satisfaction of behaving well, and that is the one satisfaction I can never do without. So shut up. As a matter of fact, I do not feel in the least inclined to worry. In any case, delightful as she is from a purely biological point of view . . .'

'Ah, yes. . . .'

'. . . Yet it is whole women that we seek, both you and I. Women delightful from a biological point of view are not unknown to us. Just now it is a person we are confronting and not a potential fountain of sensations. A person. A whole woman or one that I at least would see whole. Come on. I'm getting up.'

I stretched myself and got up, went to the bathroom and shaved and returned, did a little more stretching, dressed and went down to breakfast. I was alone. Mrs. Nance and Mr. John had already breakfasted. Miss

Sophie hadn't come down yet. I enjoyed my breakfast. The day was already warm. The servant girl moved about with considerably less than her own heaviness and poured out my coffee without spilling a drop. Birds were chattering at the window.

Sophie did not come down. I heard her calling down the front stairs, calling for breakfast to be taken up to her room. And I heard the servant girl bustling around me collecting things on a tray and humming loudly as if she liked to take Miss Sophie's things up to her. Perhaps it was nice to stand and talk for a moment in a pretty, young lady's bedroom and imagine it your own and that you too were having your breakfast in bed. I smiled round at the servant girl as she went out with Sophie's tray, and she said it was bra'e, handsome weather we were having.

After breakfast I went up and gave Mrs. Nance her massage. I had difficulty not to keep stopping to listen for signs of Sophie's movement about the house, but I felt the virtue running strong in my fingertips.

It was when I left Mrs. Nance and came downstairs that John caught me to broach the subject of Amity Nance again.

I was stepping out of the front door into the garden. John Madron was standing just outside the front door smoking his pipe.

'Good morning,' he said.

'Good morning.'

'Heavenly day again, isn't it? Not so good for the land, though. They want rain. Oh, yes. I knew there was something to ask you, Mr. Dunkel. Do you do that business of talking into somebody's hand? You know . . .'

'The manual alphabet?'

'I suppose. Yes. For people who are both—er . . .'

'It's just the same as the ordinary, one-hand deaf language, except that a blind person touches your hand as you do it.'

'Well, we have a little blind cousin, you know. Amity Nance. She lives up at Falmouth. Auntie was thinking it would be nice to have her down here. Up at Falmouth she's only got her teacher who can do this business. Auntie thinks you could broaden her horizon. Do you mind broadening people's horizons? I mean, you wouldn't have to be living in each other's pockets or anything. As a matter of fact, I believe Amity can't talk for more than a few minutes at a time to anybody but her teacher. It seems to exhaust her. You know . . .'

'Yes.'

John chugged at his pipe and mustered up the right degree of airiness in his voice.

'Well, what do you think, Mr. Dunkel?'

'I think it would be lovely.'

'I'm so glad. We all do. Only you're rather a special guest, if I may say so. I'll leave you if I may now. . . .'

And off he went to tell Mrs. Nance it was all right, and she could write to Falmouth. I listened to his footsteps as he went indoors and then pulled out a handkerchief and wafted away the tobacco fumes that he had left. A certain acidity in Master John's voice this morning, I thought. And I wondered what it was. The Rose Gwavas police force wasn't after me for pinching Sophie already, surely? I tried to remember if there had been

101

any little aloofness on Mrs. Nance's part this morning. No, surely not? It would take more than that to get under Mrs. Nance's skin. Dear, good woman. Even if she did send John to get my consent to Amity's coming. I smiled. I was filled with a sense of the luxuriousness of life. I didn't mind Amity Nance. I didn't mind even if Rose Gwavas began to secrete jealousy against me without cause. It was the right setting for a fine work of love, polite and leisured, and protected by a reasonable affluence, spring weather and isolation from all those more serious political and other matters which in London distract the mind from sufficiently votive concentration upon a single, chosen object. Desolate, bright places. I walked away with a tapping shoe-toe to the farthest part of the gardens where there were young calves breathing sweetly over the low, granite walls and where the sound of the sea could be distinctly heard.

I wondered what Sophie would find to delight me with to-day.

I did not meet her until the afternoon. She was out on some errand or other and did not come in to lunch. I sat out on the lawn reading in the afternoon. A little before tea I heard Sophie's quick feet scattering the gravel and trembled inwardly to know what she was going to say.

She was leaning over the back of my deck-chair, fingering the braille page.

'Bless you,' she said.

It was a little, whispered voice. I turned my head sideways and let it press into her belly. For a moment her fingertips strayed lightly and as it were breathlessly to the back of my hand. It was she who trembled. And then she was gone. I listened to her going and tried to turn back to my reading, but could not.

I did not find her alone at all in the evening. After supper everybody stayed downstairs to listen to something good on the wireless. I forget what it was. A play of some kind, I think. I did not listen to it. I listened to the infrequent signs that Sophie Madron was indeed in the room, to a clearing of her throat, a tip-toeing to the door and whispering to the servant girl about coffee, a setting out and pouring of the coffee when it came and at last a whispered good night and a kissing of Mrs. Nance's forehead as Sophie Madron went off to bed before the play or whatever it may have been was over.

I said:
'There was a young man I knew. He used to be a disciple of mine, used to come and sit at my feet and talk to me about all manner of things as if it helped him to deal with them. I remember the way he talked about a girl he was in love with. He said he wanted to reach her with his body torn, to be flayed, to have eaten nothing for a month, but only to have suffered pain and been tired and to bathe himself. And then at last, he said, he wanted to take off his clothes and come to her through a bed of nettles.'
That was the night after.
Sophie said:
'A little self-conscious, don't you think?'
She was kneeling beside the very low, wide bed with

her clothes beside her. I was lying belly downwards on the bed with my face towards her and one hand fallen over the edge and lost among her own hands that lay folded upon her tense, kneeling thighs.

'It was his way of knowing how,' I said.

'Knowing . . .?'

'. . . How ready you've got to be. They refine all kinds of things for use. Oil, dripping, woollen fibre, drinking water. Why not sensation? People don't use their sense of touch at all until they fall in love.'

'Except you.'

'Most people don't. And so when they come to make love it's nothing but an awful, cloying sweetness, and they don't really like it, only pretend to, and try to dodge it by a lot of unnecessary activity, hard work. . . .'

'Mm. . . .'

'. . . And mistake vigorous exercise for passion.'

It was a crazy moment. John had gone out after supper, and Mrs. Nancy had retired early. It had been difficult just to sit in front of the fire, flairing each other. And so we had found ourselves automatically leading each other by the hand upstairs and undressing each other. It had been no good. I think it had almost been meant to be no good, a deliberate try-out to see what the difficulties were that would have to be set right.

They were easy.

Sophie had acquired bad habits with a previous, stupid lover. I had come across it before. Sophie had got into the way of wanting to do the work herself, exerting her body rhythmically instead of making herself and her response completely helpless. It was impossible. That sort of thing can only be dealt with by main force, for you can't explain things while you're in the middle of them. It's indecent. And so I'd eased away from her, made her relax and smoke a cigarette, and then I'd tried to explain. It didn't matter. Of course she'd been a bit upset at first and tried to make a crying matter of it, but Sophie was much too sound to be taken in by herself to that extent.

I'd tried to explain, and then I'd made her laugh. Now we just talked.

When they've really made up their minds how things stand, and that they'd better stay as they are for the time being, two people can play with each other while they're still what is called unsatisfied, and do it without getting in the least worked up. That's how it was with us just now. I reached both hands out of bed and cupped Sophie's strenuous, clear breasts and strained my hands down her sides and let them bear my weight down where the skin distended itself upon the marvellous, braced structure of her knees and thighs as she knelt there, and presently got out of bed and put my hands to the soles of her feet and kissed her neck and shoulders and down her back and put my hands under her armpits and between her clenched buttocks and the heel of her ankles and kissed every inch of her and let my face lie in the dark, tensile hair. I wanted no more now. And only that curiously medical, romantic view which looks on love as an irresistible urge and a quantity that has to be got rid of as promptly and as regularly as possible will fail to understand how this could be as it was and be utterly delightful and sufficient and that all the rest

105

could wait on its day and hour, and be all the rarer for waiting, and all the more free of ruth or relenting.

Sophie got up and left me crouching at her feet, with my hands to her knees, and stretched herself and yawned.

'Let's go for a bathe,' she said.

'I think so, yes.'

'It will be cold,' she said, 'in April.'

'Speaking as a doctor, that is precisely what I recommend at the moment for both of us.'

I moved my hands up to her hips and pressed my cheek into her belly and pulled myself up to my feet.

We hunted for towels and walked out over Rose Gwavas heath and down into the nearest cove. It took us half an hour. I was a little irked for a while by the massive, granite enclosure of the little cove and the great rocks under water. I could have wished for open beach. I had to be told by Sophie where I could and where I could not dive. But we swam out to a little islet where a pious hermit had once lived and now only seagulls, patches of short grass and thrift and frail, bulbous campions. The moon was up. Nothing will convince me but that I can feel moonlight. There seems to be no rational justification for the belief, but lunatics and the tides, women's bodies and the howling of dogs obey the moon, and I see no reason why the faint, oppressively chill sensation I often feel at night should not be the effect of moonlight. It was, at any rate, a lucid, untroubled hour with its own magic which I could feel. Sophie was a good swimmer, better in some ways than myself, and we gave ourselves joyously, lingeringly to the sting of the April water and knew a first communion that I remem-

106

ber still in the shrill, precise tones of its poignancy.

The salt, tremulous flesh of Sophie's body, as we came out of the water, was antiseptic to all troubles of the mind. I dried her with my towel and then so kissed and caressed her that while I then heartily towelled and dressed myself she was able to stand up warm and tingling, naked without a tremor, to a rapture of night air that still had the touch of frost upon it.

She said:

'I shall go and stay at Chy Tralee for a day or two. . . .'

For a moment I shied at her.

'. . . Yes, I think I should do that. Louis. . . .'

She put a hand down to my head.

'I'm not ready yet,' she said. 'I'm not sure of myself. And if I'm seeing you about the house all day and troubling your peace of mind and you troubling mine. . . .'

I put my mouth to her thigh just above the knee.

'It's perfectly true,' I said.

And so it was. But for her to be solemn about it like that might be a danger. I wanted her not to think about it, simply to accept the way things went.

'It's perfectly true,' I said. 'Things are all coming about in impossible rotation. I half know what you're like without any clothes, and I haven't the slightest idea what you're like with your clothes on.'

She accepted the change of key.

'That's easy. I look like a fashion plate. I'm last year's fashionable brunette.'

'Slinky. . . .'

'A bit slinky. Slick, at any rate. You ought to see. In New York I did some posing for the advertisements. I've

107

got a little more up here since then, but I'm sure I could do it again if I went off potatoes. And if I had the clothes now . . .'

'They call it streamlined?'

'As bright as paint and as cheap. Acrid and cheap like cigarette smoke. Only cigarette smoke is blonde, I suppose.'

'And alkaline.'

'I'm a fatal, slinky quadroon, with slanting eyes and a hat on one side of her head. I'm sure you'd say. . . . Louis, I'm terribly young. I am. And I turn my toes in. Oh, Louis . . .'

Her flesh was beginning to chill and her teeth to chatter and the sensitive skin to come up in a gooseflesh. I felt for her sandals and buckled them to her wet feet on the pitted, wet granite.

'I'll go in the morning,' she said. 'And we'll meet somewhere outside, the day after to-morrow, in the afternoon.'

CHAPTER SIX

THIS WAS THE FIRST time I had been outside Rose Gwavas by myself. It was difficult. A dog ran out of a farm gate at me, rolling its tongue in its throat. That was unusual. After a preliminary bark or two dogs usually leave me alone until I call them. This one was nasty. It came out growling and I knew with its lip pulled back. It didn't stay. I bent for a stone, and after a little movement forward which brought its hot breath on the back of my hand it scuttled off. But I hated it and almost hated the day. The other difficulties were those of finding the way down. I had to go through Trevillian, down the Trevillian hill to the first houses in Pentreath, then break off through the village, down one of the steep, narrow streets of condemned cottages and out on the cliff just by the Gilded Lamb. I had a stick with me, like one of those blind men who go tapping along the London streets, but most of the time there was nothing to tap, and I twice landed up on the grass bank at the side of the road, once with my foot in the ditch which had fortunately run dry or almost dry. That time I sat down for a while and tried to keep my temper down and make a clear picture of the rest of the way. A van passed, and I was tempted to ask for a lift. I did not. I sat on the grass bank and fingered all the things growing there,

bird's eyes and stitchwort and a few late violets, young
nettles that could hardly sting yet, but reminded me of
the way I had talked to Sophie the night before last. I
got up and touched something I didn't like with my foot.
I kept still for a moment and then bent down and let my
fingers know. It was an adder flattened across the middle
by a car and with a lot of blood spread like thick wax on
the road. Mostly it was dead, but when I touched it near
the tail it coiled out straight and then back again to its
original recoil of death. I pushed it into the ditch with
my foot.

When I got through Trevillian it was easier. There
were more cars or vans passing, which gave me a kind
of sound-track to follow as they plunged down the
Trevillian hill into Pentreath and on towards Gwavas.
And the wall ran low and close on the road here so that
I was able to hold my stick out sideways and let it trail
along the stones. Two or three children came running
up behind me and thought I was crazy or drunk in the
middle of the day and followed me jeering and at last
came running past me and then saw what I was and
slowed down and fell silent and went almost on tip-toe,
but got a long way in front of me as quickly as they
could without even whispering a word to each other.

I passed a church with a little, worn cross let into the
granite wall. It would never go smooth like other stones,
and there was a little Christ or some earlier god on it
with arms, head and legs all the same length.

From this point there was a clear view over Gwavas
Bay. I call it a view because there isn't a nearer word. I
mean that I was suddenly exhilarated by the air that rose

110

up from Gwavas Bay without either mound or dwelling to break it, and that all of a sudden I heard the clangour and cries of Pentreath harbour and the scream of gulls rising up in a cloud from the fish market and some of them rising up high and calling in the air high above the level I was down to. I was feeling easier now.

I turned off Trevillian Hill and came through the top half of Pentreath where the new, dusty building estate was beginning to destroy the sky-line from below. I had to ask my way a little farther on. There was a corner with four or five roads off it.

Two or three men were talking there, burring the words off their tongues, and I got a whiff of poetry like a fine smell from a hot kitchen. One of the men kept on brushing the road. I suppose that was his job. He was telling the other men about the fine potatoes they grew down below Kingdom Come.

"Es,' he said, 'when they rose up and come away in their bloom. . . .'

'Excuse me,' said I. 'Which road do I take to get down to the Gilded Lamb?'

Another of the men told me. I turned away.

The road-sweeper seemed to be the poet, and as I turned away he was saying:

"Es, boy, 'tis handsome down there and all they shores. . . .'

Kingdom Come was only about five miles away, but the other men didn't seem to know it at all, and the road-sweeper might only have been there once on a holiday.

I didn't have to find my way down to the cliff. I went

111

a few yards towards the head of my little, steep street of condemned cottages and was finding the way round an iron hand-rail when I heard a footstep coming up the hill towards me that nearly stopped my heart from beating, although I had not been impatient for it till now.

Sophie did not seem to be surprised that I should recognise her without a word, and I was glad for that because I thought it showed how marvellously single she was at bottom and how easily she lived underneath the few, superficial traces of anxiety of mind. We met. She turned and walked at my side, and we came down to the cliff without saying a word to each other, sending little, loose stones running down the very steep street by themselves. Sophie was a little out of breath with first climbing up the street to meet me. On the cliff we stood in front of the Gilded Lamb to wait for a bus into Gwavas, where we should take another bus to go out to St. Guardian's. Mr. Richards, the landlord of the Gilded Lamb, was standing out against the railing over the harbour. He and Sophie exchanged remarks on the weather and Mr. Richards's vegetables and the possibility of rain. I asked Sophie how Jess and the pups were faring, and she seemed, I thought, not very interested now but told me they were doing very well. All the pups had been given away except one bitch, and Jess hardly bothered about that one any longer. The bus came, nearly getting itself wedged in with a private car in the narrows, and we climbed in.

Sophie said:

'It's May Day, Louis.'

She said it in a sunny, nature-loving way that I wanted to kill.

'In every city of Europe,' I said, 'armies are parading on behalf of peace and demonstrating their readiness to destroy each other on behalf of that vital commodity. In Hyde Park thousands of Communists, Fascists and Christians of more than one denomination are massed with banners around platforms on which their demagogues lead them in clamouring for liberty, a quantity upon the nature of which they differ considerably. And in the gardens of the wealthy, children are dancing around the Maypole, a symbol of fertility, male and erect, to advertise the profession of their dancing mistresses and teachers of deportment.'

'I know. . . .'

And she sighed.

'. . . But this morning I went out and found the fresh bracken, Louis, and took it back to Chy Tralee before breakfast. They gave me a bowl of cream, and I ate it all.'

'Is that a May Day custom too?'

'If you take a piece of hawthorn in bloom or a piece of fresh bracken to the dairy on May morning and it's long enough to go round the big, earthen bowl they give you a bowl of cream. The hawthorn's out, but I looked for the bracken. It's less flamboyant, and it takes more looking for. It's to keep the witches off the cows, I think. They're very plentiful at this time of year.'

'*Walpurgis Nacht,* to-night.'

'They'll be riding about all night on broomsticks and pitchforks.'

And I still felt for some reason or other irritated.

It may have been that I was afraid of Sophie assuming her pretty, schoolmistress rôle again, but I do not think so. I think it went deeper and at the same time wider of the mark than that. I thought there was some conflict still going on in Sophie's mind, and I didn't feel quite up to coping with it. It had been difficult coming down here alone to meet her, and that had momentarily afflicted me, no doubt, with pity for myself and resentment against things in general. Only a trace of it, but enough to concentrate me upon myself and leave me with too little energy for dealing with outside things. I thought Sophie's making a business of May Day traditions might be an attempt to cover up the political May Day which belonged for her with a proletarian, class-conscious lover. It was part of the attempt to put him aside and prepare herself for me, but I did not want to be involved with these things to-day. I wondered for a moment where Nicky Polgigga lived, what he was like and whether I should one day meet him. I hoped not. He would, I supposed, be working at the quarries this afternoon, half-choked with dust and in danger of miner's phthisis, and Sophie was thinking about him privately, perhaps unhappily, at any rate in a corner of her mind to which I had no access. So I thought. And she was still capable of taking her Celtic twilight seriously, feeling involved with it and wanting me to take it seriously too, and I would not. I shied at her. There was only one thing I wanted to be taken seriously just now, and it was, I suppose, myself. I sulked. I feel sure I sulked. And I went through my paces without conviction at first and felt very little pleasure in the afternoon.

The country around St. Guardian's is full of archæological remains. We did three of them that day.

The well at St. Guardian's Church Town was supposed to be our destination. But we got out of the bus about half a mile before that to examine the Mên-an-Tol or holed stone and the Twelve Maidens.

The Mên-an-Tol is a great ring of granite like a millstone balanced on its side on a great slab of the outcropping of granite on a hill-side overlooking St. Guardian's Church Town.

'You have to crawl through it,' said Sophie.

'For luck?'

'To be rid of pains in the back and limbs, rickets in children, and if you do it three times against the sun for scrofula.'

"I'm not scrofulous.'

But I had to go through the ring once, enduring its unresilient grip upon my ribs.

'In the name of the Father, Son and Holy Ghost,' said Sophie. 'But, of course, you only say that if it's for consumption. . . .'

She paused, and I remember the quietness and heat of the sun and the distant cries of sheep borne to us on a very light breeze.

'. . . Do you remember where I met you, Louis?'

'This afternoon?'

'Yes, at the corner there?'

'Yes.'

'That was Skipper Tre'veneth's house. . . .'

She waited as if for me to ask about it. I didn't ask.

'. . . Beth Tre'veneth had a consumption. . . .'

But she did not tell me about Beth Tre'veneth that afternoon.

'. . . It's a lovely house,' she said. 'The Adam brothers are supposed to have built it.'

And then she crawled through the Mên-an-Tol herself.

I do not know why it should have been at this point that my temper improved. It may have been the pure absurdity of crawling through ancient stones to conform with a ritual long forgotten. Or it may have been the releasing muscular effort of pulling myself through. It may have been that I helped Sophie through and in doing so had her moving and clear in my arms for a moment. I don't know. I may have left some ailment of my own on the Mên-an-Tol. Although I am blind I am no doubt still capable of blindness, and there may have been some of that left on the granite when I crawled through.

The Twelve Maidens are pillars of hewn granite in a circle. The legend is that twelve young girls from St. Guardian's were turned to stone while dancing here on a Sunday when they should have been in church. If you embraced one of the stones at midnight at the time of the full moon it would come to life again in your arms. Sophie assured me that this was a Christian fabrication to make people forget their own dangerous past. This had obviously been a temple of the Druids or even an Iberian temple of the time before there had been any Druids. It seemed likely enough. But their mass of stone is oppressive, and I was more interested in Sophie. It struck me now, as we leaned against one of the great pillars of granite, that I had no right to question her mood any more than her memory, that she had quietly ignored my tendency to sulk, where a commonplace woman might have turned apologetic and suggested not coming this way after all if it did not interest me, and that I ought similarly to ignore what I took to be her tendency to phantasy worship of the Cornish, her racial past, and let her work it out of herself in her own way.

Perhaps this little pilgrimage was for her the stages of a ritual of initiation and therefore practical, after all, like my young friend's imaginary bed of nettles. In which case I must not merely accept but indeed encourage it.

I found the critical, blind mood had left me with a headache.

'Put your finger there,' I said.

She put the tip of her index finger between what I must still call my eyes.

'Can you feel the nerve throbbing?'

'Yes,' she said.

"That's how I make my living. I feel where the nerves are throbbing and then persuade them not to.'

'I've cured a headache myself before today.'

It cured mine now just to have Sophie Madron's finger there. We both leaned against the same great pillar of granite, she with her finger to a throbbing, concentrated nerve. It was very hot and still. The granite pillar was hard. Grooved, massive and hard, comfortless and un-yielding to the touch. I thought this hill was perhaps a very holy place, but I preferred humanity. I felt the stuff of Sophie Madron's dress with my fingers. It was a heavy, fine cotton.

117

'What colour is it?'

'Red and white, a lot of flowers printed on it in red.'

I touched her hat. It was a neat, shallow straw, with a gallant curve to it.

'White?'

'Yes.'

'And you're very dark?'

'Yes.'

'The sun shines through the brim of your hat and makes a pattern on your face?'

'I can't see.'

'And you look terribly, terribly cool?'

'I hope.'

Her dress had sleeves to just above the elbow. I felt how very smooth her forearm was and moved a hand to her top lip to find her prefectly hairless there too. She had open-worked gloves on and carried a light, flat bag with its strap over a delicate wrist.

'You're terribly smart for a country walk.'

I had to touch her. I have to touch, as another man will look. I put the mere tips of my fingers to her buttocks, to her breasts and on her belly, and found no articles of female machinery there. Her clothes slid smoothly on perfect clarity of body. I knelt to find her ankles and feet. She had no stockings on. Her legs were perfectly smooth too, with very delicate bone at the ankles, and her feet were cool in their sandals among the harsh, dry blades of moorland grass which the wind did not stir.

'Don't touch me very much just now,' she said.

And the sigh on which she said it indicated absolute

contentment. Her finger was still in the same place, bemusedly resting there as I had knelt and as I now stood up again.

We walked off down the hill towards St. Guardian's Church Town, a hamlet of eight or ten houses and a church. The well is an overgrown cleft between stones, where a trickle of water runs only a few yards below.

'St. Guardian is not a Christian saint at all. He is Hu Gadarn, the Celtic deity. King Arthur was a later, popular version of the same divine person.'

Sophie announced just so much in a mechanical, guidebook voice and was evidently enclosed within the circle of her own thoughts, and at the same time very much closer to me or I to her for the contact of a few minutes ago.

I knew that she was nearly ready for me.

I tried to picture her as she was in solitude, the hour to hour tranquillity of these last two days up at Chy Tralee. She had that lovely, incomprehensible numbness upon her in which a woman can let things done with subside and things to come burgeon of themselves without the operation of her will, in a manner that men are incapable of as indeed are many, denatured women. I felt something like religious awe in her presence now, and wondered if I ought to be with her at all in this tranced, female solitude of hers. I remembered in my fingers the drying, waxy blood of an adder and thought that certainly I should not have touched her with the same fingers, though touch I must. I wanted to lead her away and take her back to Chy Tralee, and stealthily leave her there without another word spoken between us.

Down by the sea an hour later she was telling me what I knew.

'I'm nearly ready for you, Louis. Another two days, if you'll wait. . . .'

I did not touch her now.

It is a strange thing, this numbness of a woman withdrawn into herself for purgation and renewal. It is a complete withdrawal from the world, and it leaves her apathetic even towards the person for whom she would be renewed.

'And you,' she said. 'Are you all right?'

'Yes. . . .'

I was ashamed to find that I had been taking it all less seriously than she. But I was all right. I did not doubt it.

'I'll come to you at exactly a quarter to twelve the night after to-morrow. When there's nobody about,' she said. 'And you meet me outside. Come out on the heath to meet me. Yes. It doesn't matter, but perhaps if the nights have turned warmer by then with the turn of the moon . . .'

Awful, awful solemnity. I think I must have trembled through and through. And I cannot but have hated it.

She wanted to travel back to Mrs. Tralee's by herself now. I let her go. I sat on a rock down by the sea. It was out beyond Pengenno Cove. I sat there like a stranded merman and listened to Sophie Madron stepping over the rocks towards the village inland, and presently lit a cigarette, and shortly after it another, and presently a third.

I did not wish to stay about the house all day, waiting

120

for that night. Nor did I wish to do anything strenuous and risk jading myself. I thought the pleasantest thing would undoubtedly be to drive out with John, and I put my mind to the invention of some means of persuading John that it was the thing to do. I did not want to get at him by way of Mrs. Nance. He was probably hating me enough already for being Auntie's pet. I thought perhaps if I looked lost enough, picking up books and putting them down, opening the piano and closing it again, he might respond. He did. And it was not out of mere politeness. He was feeling lost himself, I thought, and he seemed to be keyed up, agitated about something. He did not, in fact, talk to me about himself, but I think he would have done so with a couple of pints of beer and a little more encouragement.

He had only one pint of beer, at the Red Lion in Truro. I paid for John's lunch, and he was ready enough to talk over coffee in the Red Lion lounge, but I did not lead him on, and the beer was not strong enough in him.

All the same, it was contact. We arranged ourselves on the best of terms, though I felt the occasional movements of suspicion in John's mind. It was in fact a highly delightful day. After a while John was driving for the simple pleasure of driving, and that was good. We drove up to the north from Truro and then down that coast, and had the Atlantic and the Irish Sea air with us, as freshening as the air on the south coast could be enervating, sharp-fractured slate as against the southern, carnelian-streaked granite, air like silk, where the other was often like velvet. The sea was more boisterous here, thundering and hooting through funnels in the rock and falling back in perpetual cascade. It was a male sea. Down at Pentreath I have felt the sea come lolling up from the Bay of Biscay, flowing here into Gwavas Bay and on through the Channel, deeply breathing, momentarily spent, yet infinitely powerful, as a woman breathes when she's been loved better than well. I thought John enjoyed the male, northern sea here as he could not enjoy the more sullen, heavy waters to the south. I think he was probably a very sensitive man in his puzzled, inhibited way, and have wondered since whether he ever took to writing poetry or music in secret, or whether his only outlet were in fantasies of love and war.

He told me one or two anecdotes of the time when Sophie and he had lived in a small house up on this coast with their parents before their father had divorced his wife and taken the two of them to America, and presently died. They were insignificant anecdotes, to the effect that it was at this point where Sophie had been caught by the tide at the age of four, and here on this other headland that John himself had broken a leg while hunting for sea-birds' eggs, but I learned something about Sophie from them.

I learned, for instance, that their father's interests had been archæological, and that in the intervals of his professional labours as an historian he had tried, with some others, to revive the Cornish language, and to institute a Gorsedd and various other bardic and other druidical ceremonies here in Old Cornwall after the pattern of Morien in Wales. I thought this of importance to my understanding of Sophie, because it linked up her own passages of Celtic reminiscence with the love of her father and showed me, if dangerous they were, in just what corner of her world the danger lay. John also had the flair, but he had repressed it more deeply than Sophie. He told me one item of archæological interest with direct reference to his sister, and it was that archæologists were now beginning to agree that the Mongolian strain in the British Isles had been concentrated in Cornwall as nowhere else. And didn't I think it showed in Sophie? I did. I thought it fitted her far more closely than Mrs. Nance's vague, popular ascription of Spaniard or Jew, or the faint suggestion of American Creole girl that Sophie herself cultivated, no doubt because it was in America that she had first become conscious of her own person. I thought the lightly waxen, perfectly hairless texture of her, the miraculous, ageless precision of flesh and bone in Sophie's body, and the deep, slanting planes of her face might well have been the Mongol in our midst.

Not that it mattered. It was a Mongolian strain, like that of Old Russia, subjected to countless generations of other breeding and refinement till it remained no more than as a faint, ancestral excitement and a hiding place for reserves of both sensuality and extreme fastidiousness which I knew were there already without the Mongolian suggestions of the archæologist.

There were other things, too, that I learned, and some of them were more immediately important.

We got back to Rose Gwavas only a little before supper, but in time to bathe and drink our sherry slowly. I tingled from the air, and Mrs. Nance assured me that I was already thoroughly sunburnt. Mrs. Nance was in a

123

notably happy frame of mind that evening, perhaps because I and her John had at last made a thing of it together.

And then I was out in the night air waiting. It was still chilly. I did not see any possibility of love being propitiated to-night by a bed of moss and ferns beneath the open sky. It would have to be a closed room. And on the whole I was rather glad. Despite the insects and other possible intruders, afternoon love in the sunlight can be very sweet when it is there to be had. And a night of stars has no doubt its glamour for those who can see them, as it certainly has the most delicate odours and sounds. All the same, a room is my choice. I was brought up in a provincial town, where country lanes and parks are the only rendezvous of love. I did not rent any flat of my own until I was twenty-five, and without eyes to see, and the privacy of a room had become far more glamorous to me by that time than any open air.

Sophie had enjoyed a more sophisticated upbringing.

And in any case I was meeting her in the open air, and she would rest for a while in my arms beneath the open sky before I presently led her away to her own room. That was a place to be loved. I remembered the quietness and simplicity of the room and that Sophie had been absent from it three nights, the diadem of jewels from its case. It was the place for me. I would lead her there. To-morrow it was there I should awake, and she would be lying happily assuaged beside me in the warmth of the morning sun. I trembled. The facetious

124

mood in which I have thought that love is best approached would not stay with me now.

I had at last allowed myself to become impatient.

The scents of the Rose Gwavas gardens became more poignant every moment under the sting of the night air, until the inner edges of my nostrils tingled. I found a scented geranium, and I found southernwood. The fine down behind leaves excited my fingers. In the great trees a mighty work was in process, for neither oak nor ash had leaved themselves as yet. The faint, disturbing vestiges of sight began to awaken in my head. Things as I passed them by had a visible form, and the woman coming towards me soon was a ghostly, white vision of adolescence. I would not see. I listened. Owl, badger and fox, a night-jar crying. I wondered if the nightingale sang down here. I came out of the gardens on to Rose Gwavas heath. Insects and frogs were busy in the two or three acres of marsh. A farm lay only a hundred yards to my left, and I caught the wood-smoke and the restlessness of stalled cattle. Along the nearest road a little farther away telephone wires were singing.

It was not so far from twelve o'clock. I thought not of English witches, nor of their older, divine ancestors and the cauldron of inspiration. In any case, *Walpurgis Nacht* was over now. I thought of other magic of an actual, demonstrable world.

The sun was only going down on the first islands of the west, and on Greenland waking from the ice, and people there were turning from their labours and seeking either pleasure or rest. Throughout the continent of the Americas it was still broad daylight. A hard, electrical life was lived there, or an indolent, dissatisfied life in the southerly regions. But the sun was travelling hard west, leaving the American continent for Japan and for agonised China, and for many islands of the south, and the everlastingly virginal, still unawakened Australasian lands. At Bombay, at Samarkand and at the gates of European Russia the dawn was breaking over hill and valley, sliding across the misty plains. It would travel back through night-ridden, secretly planning Europe and reach me here again in only a few hours. Only a few, but they were hours of leisurely delight. In countless cities of Europe lovers were reaching out of the darkness of sleep to exchange their proper merchandise one with another. Some were lying restlessly alone, troubled by the languor of May, spring weather. And soon it would be my turn. Slower than the sun, but more unerringly quick, she was coming across farmland and heath, stepping lightly with a fearful, glad heart and senses already quickened.

I felt sick with this new impatience. Then the sickness was gone, and there was the feeling of religious awe again, creeping through me like a physical drugging of the senses, a paralysis of nerve and limb that I could not withstand.

Humility in passion, awful, over-solemn anticipation. I could not bear it. I was not a boy. Sophie had me waiting for her like a sick, adolescent boy. And I would not endure it. I shook my head. I dragged myself more fully erect and breathed in at the uttermost depth, distended my nostrils and induced in myself semblances of the arrogance that I wanted. So I should meet her, arrogant,

126

male and indifferent, and then let the tenderness enter into me later. I was the active, deftly adjusted male. It was for Sophie to make herself recipient and gather herself beneath a cloud of thought and vision.

A step rustling the dead, last year's bracken, dislodging a pebble. I waited until my ears had her whereabouts in focus and then stepped forward and held the living, heavily breathing girl in my arms, leaning full of sighs, as it seemed, against me.

Then withdrawing.

And the breathless, metallic voice saying:

'Oh. Oh. . . . Was that intended for me?'

I squirmed. And then I laughed.

'No,' I said. 'But it was extremely pleasant all the same.'

Betty des Voeux laughed too. She stood for a moment as if waiting for what came next. Then off she went.

'Sorry,' I called out.

'Not at all. . . .'

I cursed her. Then I laughed again. It was better than the awful, highly-strung waiting of a moment ago. I ought to be thankful to the woman. A moment ago I had been liable to emotional displacement that might quite well have spoilt the night for both of us, both Sophie and myself.

Betty des Voeux was coming to John to-night, was she? I felt friendly towards her. And towards John. I chuckled. There would be the four of us in two, nearly adjacent rooms, lifting the roof off Rose Gwavas with our miscellaneous ardour. I thought we ought to have made up a square party, or at any rate, laid a bet as to which of us made the best night of it.

I would not tell Sophie, though.

And now it was truly she, coming towards me. And I did not think of anything else, but of her.

She was perfectly quiet and still, more perfectly grave, better prepared for me than I for her. Or perhaps it was the same with her as with me, and she had been like me, full of incipient panic, alternating between violent extremes of mood until this moment at which again we came face to face. It was, I suppose, the perfect readiness, each to be the counterpoise of the other, lost and a prey to emotion each by himself, then coming together again, utterly tranquil in that instant as the single magnetic field restored itself and functioned again in our meeting.

We did not kiss or touch at all out here.

'Hello,' said Sophie.

And that was all. I turned and walked with her over the heath and back into the grounds of Rose Gwavas and into the house. I plucked off leaves of the myrtle to fill both hands as she opened the door and went in.

In the hall we kissed. And then straight up to her room we went together.

I think I loved her that night as well as any woman may be loved while the love is still watchful, half a matter of wooing and only half of unconsiderable passion. It was very quickly made known that indeed it was love and not a hopeful illusion, and as the night grew towards inevitable morning all reservations of the mind seemed to have long been down. Only the physical imperfection of those who do not as yet know each other completely well remained with us, and that is always left in part even after a month or a year, certainly never evaded until a man has followed the cycle of the moon, twice, three times, as it plays on the woman's body, rousing, impeding and again releasing her, in the perpetual, tidal flow of her life, which is not still for a moment throughout all the years of her womanhood, five and thirty years, the half of three score and ten.

A man's potency also is never at rest. It increases over a period of months or in a different man of weeks, and then subsidies for a while until the increase will begin again. And perhaps a man never reaches the height of his potency all his life. For it lives only as it is called into play by this particular woman or that, and is at one time sterile and another fertile, and may turn itself into other, wasteful or conservative channels or lie for a long time in a kind of recession which also may be either conservative or wasteful.

It is liberated in the act of love or in the sleep after love, or in the days which are superficially days of tedium, irritation and mistrust, or while a man lies awake at night and reflects on the sleeping woman beside him, curiously, without immediate passion, enquiring into the sources of her life and the meaning of those many years before he found her as a lover.

CHAPTER SEVEN

TO-NIGHT SHE was her father's daughter. To-morrow or the night after that she would have changed and become her own, unique self again. Or it would be some other man out of the past who momentarily displaced her personality, concentrated the muscles about her forehead, made a pattern for the manner and the need, in which at length she would turn to me, and cried out in every gesture of her body to be exorcised and laid more perfectly to rest. To-night it was her father who stirred within her and would not let her come awake free and untroubled, belonging altogether to me.

She lay curled up like a child in the womb. Her features were relaxed, but one hand pressed against her belly and the other flung aslant across the pillow. Every now and then it was as if she had stopped breathing. Then she turned, still with the one, vague hand to her belly and the other wandering above her head seeking where to lie, and her knees climbing up towards her breast and her shoulders arching over.

If her lips moved it would be to form the words:
'I know. Yes. Yes, I know.'

And then she would sigh with a kind of resignation. For she did not understand why her mother had to go away so often, why her father who loved his wife so much and thought of nothing but how to be kind to her, and looked so childishly trusting and contented when she came into the room, could only make her mother suffer. Only she had learnt that dear, good men hurt women. She knew. Yes. Yes, she knew. Love was a thing that caused women to be hurt. Women were there to be hurt and puzzled by love. Then at last they went away, although it was not what they wanted to do.

John hated his father. It was because he loved his mother too much. He understood even less than herself. He did not know and accept the difference between men and women. To John it was his father's wickedness that made their mother go away. He loved her foolishly, just like his father. But he did not know it. And so he raged in secret against their father and told lies about him, made up stories about how one night he had lain awake and heard their mother crying, and had crept downstairs and found his father beating her with a leash, or how, at another time, their mother had come and sat on his bed, looking like an angel from Heaven in her white, silk nightdress, but crying, holding his hand and making him swear that if anything ever happened to her he would kill their father without a moment's thought. How foolish John was, how angry and unjust. He did not know that it was just the way men were, that women were different and must be hurt by their own love. When he discovered it in part he would hate himself for being a man and for being his father's son.

I knew how it was.

Mrs. Nance had said:

'Patrick was all right, but nobody ever told him any-

131

thing. He'd read about women in poetry books and history books. Margaret Lester could have taught him a thing or two, but he didn't know wisdom came out of anything but books, and when a thing went wrong he fled to his library and searched for the truth of it there. As if the ancients knew anything about women. . . . The one thing they made a mess of themselves. . . .'

Sophie's father and John's had been Patrick Madron, Mrs. Nance's brother. Margaret Lester he'd courted and married up in Falmouth, though she wasn't a West Country girl at all.

Admiral Madron had been at sea. Patrick had stayed at home with their tired, stupid mother, reading because there was nothing else to do and nobody to tell him anything. Admiral Madron, when he came home, had found his son reading and despised him, and felt no inclination to tell him anything. The few things he knew he'd communicated to his daughter, who was Mrs. Nance.

'Margaret Lester was all right. . . .'

Only Patrick Madron hadn't learnt what it meant for a woman to be all right.

I knew what they were like, these men of refined, intellectual taste. They were passionate men, but their passion had gone astray. They loved, but what it was they loved had evaded them and take unto itself another name, as that of Mary Queen of Scots or Petrarch's Laura, Dido of the Carthaginians, or Ruth.

Once I had to interview the mother of a girl who found that for three weeks out of every month the muscles of her thighs and back were too stiff to dance with, and that during her period this stiffness became so acute that she was racked through with pains and then gradually relaxed, until for just a week she was able to dance perfectly well again. I found that the girl's mother was the wife of a university professor, and that she had all the superficial characteristics of an enlightened woman. She was perfectly frank, and talked about physiological matters without the slightest reserve and had carefully explained the facts of life to her daughter at the onset of puberty without attempting to hush up anything at all. The only thing was that the facts of life she'd explained were disinterested, biological facts designed only for the birth of children and the occasional gratification of those odd creatures called men in their more uncontrollable moments, and naturally enough the girl had found this picture of the new, adult life revolting and had revolted against it organically by clenching herself more tightly every moment against the periodical symptom of her maturity. I asked the mother if she had not at some time perhaps enjoyed sleeping with her husband, quite apart from male needs and the possibility of children.

'I beg your pardon,' she said.

I repeated my question.

The woman laughed. I believe she thought that being sightless I was full of the ideals of innocence, and that the facts of life were something quite outside my experience.

'My dear Mr. Dunkel . . .'

She explained as if to a child who would not understand in any case.

'. . . If I showed any signs of enjoying that, my husband would consider me no better than a whore.'

She did not add:

'And a whore is precisely what I should be.'

But it was evidently her thought.

Margaret Lester had not accepted the myth, although I had no doubt that like this woman she had tried to in order to avoid troubling Patrick Madron's divided, passionate mind.

And there it was, the domestic interior in which John and Sophie Madron had for the first twelve, thirteen years of their life struggled painfully towards the light.

Sophie turned again in her sleep.

A moment ago she had been with her father, a child, dark-ringleted, standing outside his study door, wanting to go in and tell her father things that she had no words for. A serious, premonitory child, already full of a piteous, dark excitement, emotionally precocious. Now she had turned away from there and was near her mother in London, a mother whose discontent had turned now to resentment and almost to hate, and who tried to hurt the father by introducing a lover, having him take the young child Sophie upon his knee. And there she was sitting upon the stranger's knee, knowing vaguely who he was, that he was a thief invited to break into their house and steal what he probably did not want, but feeling no anger or shame, not recoiling from him, only wanting to understand the sadness, the inevitable hurt.

Soon there would be the open quarrel, the scenes and the whispering relatives. Admiral Madron, her grandfather, was stumping in on his wooden leg if she remembered correctly, but the wooden leg had probably come out of a story-book, and he was making jokes in a loud voice and trying to get everybody to calm down, putting the men in a good humour. Outside, in the wood-shed, John was sitting huddled up, crying. He cried all day and would not eat, and when she'd gone and tried to put her arms round him and tell him not to mind, for it was the way of the world, he'd just hacked her shins with his heel and, at last, got up and walked off into the road and down to the sea in a vexation.

Later everybody had put on their best clothes and gone up to London for the divorce, and only her father had come back.

And then the preparations.

The letters by the morning post, bearing foreign stamps with a picture of George Washington, who never told a lie, and no Esq. after Patrick Madron, the name and address of the sender written on the envelope.

John hating the big ship, adult people walking around its deck, playing games and dancing all day.

Everybody crowding to see the Statue of Liberty.

Officials, waiting-rooms, different people with common voices. For a while they had followed their father round on his lecture tour.

It was very painful, this change-over from one life to another. She had cried a good deal herself, but quietly and without letting anybody know, until the tears had seemed to be acid and burn her inwardly.

Sophie was struggling against it. On the pillow beside me the head with its vital, caressive hair was turning from one side to the other. Her arm fell across my face.

135

I put my lips to the beating vein in its hollow and then, as she moved again, half sat up, propped on my elbow, bending over her. Out of the abysses of sleep she came, very warm, odorous and hot with sleep, stretching her arms about my neck and all her weight pulling down upon me, childishly greedy, selfish as she came from sleep, desiring to be comforted and half desiring to suffocate the comforter because he was a person and not a thing. And so I had to comfort her, giving her the semblances of adult, mated love, while she only half awakened and gave not a thought to me, but only to what her body momentarily lacked, to the more luxurious rugs that might be spread before the fire and to the subservience of any other creature that might be there.

If she had come fully awake, awake enough to observe herself, she would have been shocked, but she was only reaching out from a troubled sleep and in a short while travelling back again to a sleep that was quite untroubled.

At another time she wanted to talk.

She wanted to tell me about the past, about a previous lover, this or that stage in her erotic training. It was not that she wanted me to understand her. Not at all. At such a time I was no more to her than a further development of this erotic training, and she was taking it very seriously, very self-consciously. She was the Alexandrian courtesan, the hetaira, priestess of profane love initiating herself more ultimately into its mysteries. And I was the new priest from Antioch, her teacher. It was a play, a ritual to be enacted.

But I listened and responded for love of the actress.

'One of the masters at the school in New York . . .'

She had made her voice very simple and explanatory, rather humble, apologetic.

'. . . It was a theory in Germany at that time.'

What was?

'About older men initiating young girls at school.'

My little catechumen sat upon the edge of her bed.

'I think he was a bit in love with me.'

'And . . .?'

'He thought I was still too young. Three or four of the girls in my class slept with him. But he was rather in love with me. He didn't want to hurt me, I think.'

'You were . . .?'

'. . . Thirteen. I was very lonely. We'd only just come to New York. I didn't mix very well with the other girls. Most of them were Jewesses, and all their parents knew each other. But I was very pretty. And I was already . . .'

She moved herself off the bed and crouched at my feet.

'. . . I used to go and sit in his room sometimes to ask him questions about work. He read Heine to me, though I didn't know German very well. Sometimes I lay upon his bed, and he caressed me with his hands. He took my clothes off and dressed me again, and I didn't move. I just lay there with my eyes shut.'

Under a heavy, satin négligée she was naked, and she had much powdered, bathed and adorned her body.

'I left that school quite soon. Our father had more money after a year. I had just begun to like the school. But the girls were very excitable. They used to run about

137

in the dressing-rooms and compare their bodies with each other. Some of them used to get a piece of lipstick and draw faces on their belly or on their breasts with the nipple for a nose. I didn't like those games very much.'

I think I was her perfect listener. I sat there on the edge of her bed in pyjamas and dressing-gown, she sitting coiled up at my feet. I would have that rather majestic, benevolently wise look of Homer, Milton or Oedipus at Colonus with his daughter, or the blind face of the priest in the confessional.

'Go on, my daughter. . . .'

I accepted the part and felt myself to be full of ancient wisdom, secret knowledge. And, indeed, my absolution was sure.

'. . . I was only fourteen. He was a friend of my mother's. I went to stay with her in Palestine for the autumn. She wanted me, and my father did nothing but work. My mother's friend was a French Jew. I think she turned to Jewish people because my father was so perfectly Christian. They were living in Tel-Aviv. My mother wanted me to have this man, though I don't suppose she knew that she wanted it. It was her way of isolating my father still more. She didn't mind about John, though I think John loved our mother more than I did. He didn't seem to live at all, in those days. He spent most of his time locked up in his room at my father's apartment, and he kept falling sick.'

'But this man . . .?'

'I didn't like him very much. I saw him next year, and he'd got fatter. I think he'd probably been fat all the

138

time, but he was gentle and sensitive, and I liked love, even if I didn't very much like him. I thought I was made for love. I had awful fantasies. I wanted to be a whore. I thought it was my vocation, like taking the veil. Like taking the veil in a Jewish city instead of a Christian one. I used to walk about the streets in an awful, sensual haze and hope that some of the men would pick me up.'

'All this at the age of fourteen?'

'Yes, I was fourteen. I went to Tel-Aviv again the next autumn and stayed a whole year. I was going to college when I got back to America, and my father didn't mind very much where I went in the meantime. He loved me, but he thought I was my mother's child. I wasn't, but I think my father was afraid of me. And this time I had a boy who was only eighteen. We lived together in my mother's house. I was very much in love with him. And I think I was at my best then. I was prettier than I am now.'

My own desire began to stir within me. I hated the story now. My fingers had to stray to Sophie's face and assure me that she was scatheless and uncoarsened, without the hard, brittle distortion, the tooth of the whore. I was quickly reassured. All these things had passed through her lightly. The lines of her hand were not deeply graven. It had left no scar or callous any more than another girl's passion for a favourite mistress at school.

And yet she had been for a year crazily happy, and then she had suffered.

'It was I who had to teach him. He was clumsy and afraid. I had to show him. And yet the first time we came

139

together it was like water flowing into water.'

Her own voice had become tremulous now, tremulous and throaty. She was turning to me. It was all right now. She did not mind that I should be moved. I entered into the picture now.

'I don't think he will be happy with anybody else. I had to cut his navel string for him, and I think it will grow again. I felt so proud and important, teaching him love when I was only fifteen myself. I still felt that I was made for love. . . .'

Brutal child. For to-night again she was still a child. And the love to-night was a mathematical problem, a question in erotics. I was to lead her into a further, more ultimate court of the temple.

'. . . I did not want to be a whore that year. But I still felt that love was my vocation.'

I touched her lips to stop her talking. And I lifted her to her feet and laid her upon the bed and caressed her until she was quiet and her eyes full of tears, seeming strangely small, and as young as in her fantasy she was. I must not move her deeply to-night. The tendrils, the buds of her life were all close to the surface. It was a love gentle and nervous, gathering itself quickly to a little crisis and then without excess receding, a dance of idealised sensation, wilfully frustrating itself, like an erotic dance in the theatre where the limbs of the dancers entwine without a hold and their lips continually approach and never meet, a love without perceptible fatigue that prolonged itself imperceptibly into sleep and seemed never to have been interrupted at all when at last the morning came.

I have never found that even the most frankly pagan, transitory love was easy. A woman is at all times a continent to be explored, not a port of call. I have sometimes envied those men who are only good for love when heavily primed with drink, and fully assured that their responsibility will not be extended beyond a night, although it is certain that even that single night must always be a rather depressing experience for them, and a thing for which the only justification is their sense of liberation on the morrow.

Sophie Madron was not more difficult than any other woman taken with equal seriousness.

And yet I remember that during those early days of our acquaintance I had moments of a lassitude so heavy that I half wanted to leave her sleeping there and take myself far away out of her world.

I have listened to her breathing beside me and thought of lovers, father, mother and race, two whole, unknown continents she had lived in, and groaned:

'How many evil spirits more to be exorcised, and how many dragons to be slain before I come to her?'

And yet these dragons, the evil spirits I had encountered, were poor, unimportant creatures.

I remembered how on my first evening at Rose Gwavas, Mrs. Nance had said:

'Nobody's made enough demands on her yet to get anything coming out through the boredom. Sophie's untried.'

And although there were a great many things that she did not know of Mrs. Nance had been fundamentally right.

141

These things had slipped through Sophie's experience without being retained. In attempting to re-live them with me she was not experiencing a need to be rid of them in the process so much as to go back and capture them and integrate them into a life they had left almost completely unchanged and so become able to forget them. That had been her childhood.

Now she was a woman, and Mrs. Nance could say of her:

'She lays herself open. At the moment she's trying herself out on a young quarryman. . . . He's a blue-eyed boy, and I think it's sentimental mostly . . . .'

And to say that was almost completely true and adequate. I did not know precisely how far back these early, precocious moments lay in Sophie's experience, but certainly they were inaccessible now to anything but a vague, hopeless nostaglia of childhood. At a first encounter, she had even become stupid in love. And I fancied that between the age of sixteen and her present age, whatever it was, Sophie Madron had been as inhibited, as timid and unfree, as any other girl in her environment, until she had entered, gravely and with due concern, but unprotected by experience, into the relationship with her Nicky Polgigga.

How important this had been for her, I could not tell. It lay too near the surface yet.

Nicky Polgigga was neither a dragon nor an evil spirit yet, so far as I could see. He might become either or both, changing as he subsided into the deep places of Sophie's life, but at present one could only say of him that he was somewhere in the offing, a person somewhere in Pen-

142

treath, dreeing his weird in his own, stumbling way, rather a fool in love, defeated to date and not up to Sophie's standard, but no doubt extremely charming and very much alive.

As a matter of fact I was very conscious those first, troubled days of the young man being somewhere in the offing.

Not that Sophie made me conscious of him. She was at the moment far too busy indulging her childhood, getting rid of earlier devils, liberating herself or being liberated by me. And I did not meet her during the day except in a vague, troubled haze at lunch and supper.

It was easy to pass those days along. Life was so thoroughly mammocked at night and we so chastened by morning, that the day became a kind of aimless, delightful sleep and an interlude in which we bathed and ate, read a little and enjoyed the seemingly endless sun, apart. But we gave one night a miss. The crest of a wave not quite ready to break, the ghosts all laid, it was a necessity of personal discipline, the hygiene of love. And then to give helplessly swimming bodies to the final mounting and the breaking of the wave. For luckily Sophie was not inhibited by the Mosaic, nor by any primitive law. And it was in the evening of our day of rest, a Sunday, quite probably, that I became aware of somebody near me as I stood on the bridge in the water garden. There was a moment of absolute silence, every living thing aware of some intruder more intent than myself. And then I heard bushes being pushed aside and bracken crackling underfoot, and it was evidently not a

143

fox or a straying dog. It might have been a tramp, but I did not think so.

Port was still possible in the library, though by now I pleased myself whether I took it or not.

I went up to Mrs. Nance and sat down and mused.

'John tells me,' I said, 'that there's an Adam house in Pentreath. I didn't know the Adam brothers had ever been in Cornwall at all.'

And I got the story of Beth Tre'veneth who had lived there. And it was also Master Nicky's story, as I had thought.

Beth Tre-veneth lived in a lunatic asylum now, and only her aunt and the aunt's companion lived at the Tre'veneth house.

It seemed a little strange to me that a girl given to pulmonary tuberculosis should also suffer in her mind to such an extent. Usually madness strikes a person in one place only, in the lungs or in the stomach, in a cancerous breast or in the mind.

The story of Beth Tre'veneth was a story of losing her father, Skipper Tre'veneth, and then of being in love with Nicky Polgigga. Nicky Polgigga had a very bad conscience and thought himself cause of the madness of Beth Tre'veneth.

It was a story told in Pentreath.

And Sophie had tried to revise an old story.

The day after that we met in the morning.

After breakfast and after Mrs. Nance's massage I went out into the garden.

I thought:

'To-day will not be so easy to pass along. I did not lie with Sophie all night, and all this day I shall wait impatiently for the night to come.'

Particularly since I knew what moment this was in the rhythm of Sophie's life and that to-night I might find I had missed the best of her by an hour or two, three hours, or by the fraction of a minute.

But as I went round the side of the house and a little way up the drive to skirt the great sacrificial altar of stratified rock, I heard what I remembered hearing on the afternoon of my arrival, while I was still dazed and everything about me disturbingly new and strange. I heard Sophie talking to a kitten, and every now and then humming a few bars of tuneless, rhythmically potent blues to herself.

I thought:

'This is the last time I shall perceive her in that first, simple guise, as she was before the love and war between us modified two people and left the photographs on our passports no longer valid.'

But I didn't mind. The new image being painfully born out of the death of many old ones, had a deeper tone, more wealth and even more excitement.

Sophie heard me and waited for me to come in sight. 'Hello,' she said.

Her voice was a little apprehensive, as if in remembering a delirium and then a pause, she wondered now whether these things and herself would bear a morning scrutiny.

As for me, I was moved strangely by her unfamiliarity. The nights had a dream-like quality in the mind. I

145

remembered the intervening, aimless days.

'Hello,' I said. 'It's a long time since I saw you.'

'Yes. . . .'

And besides, it was a different she. It was herself, not her body that had been full of ghosts. This morning she was adult, queenly and free. It was the she come fresh out of her retreat at Chy Tralee. Only now she had not even the concealed, to-herself-unknown impediment that even then had flawed her. I tried to prohibit the emotion by finding phrases for her in my mind. A lovely, radiant woman. Quiet and infinitely deep, her radiant womanhood. But I could not. The breath shattered, was broken in my lungs. It was like the painful, uncontrollable shock of ice-cold water clutching at the heart.

I said without breath:

'Who are you?'

Oh, she was happy enough.

'A woman in love,' she said.

She laughed.

'Oh, Louis . . .'

Then she had two hands to my temples and was going all over my face with little, nibbling kisses. And she was telling me that she loved me, and forever would, and a dozen other nonsensical things which told me all the same that she was happy.

When she was quiet again and my hands went up to her face I found them wet with a few tears that she couldn't trouble to wipe away.

She said:

'Let us do something together.'

'Now?'

146

'Yes, all the day. Something quiet and sensible.'

'Go to some place?'

'I don't know. Yes, anything. Go to some place or read a book together. Anything. . . .'

We took the market bus from Trevillian into Gwavas and a train from Gwavas to St. Ives. We ate the joint and two vegetables at a bad hotel and bathed from separate, iodine-smelling tents and sat for a while on the beach.

'Let us be a little tired,' said Sophie.

And so we walked five miles from St. Ives to Zennor and outside Zennor paid our respects to the memory of D. H. Lawrence, and in Zennor visited the church and felt with our fingers the worn, oak body of the Mermaid of Zennor, and had tea and caught a bus away from Zennor and made our supper of bread and cheese at a public house, and so maintained together the simple, moving continuity of the day until ten o'clock, and then travelled from Gwavas to Pentreath and walked up the hill through Trevillian from Pentreath, and arrived back at Rose Gwavas when everybody was in bed and ours the freedom of the house.

Sophie said:

'I feel as if I were going to burst into song, and I know I'm not.'

We made ourselves tea in the kitchen, and sat there and drank it with perfect gravity.

CHAPTER EIGHT

I SAID TO MYSELF:

'Now she is one and indivisible, a whole.'

I said:

'Something I introduced into her life, and it split, divided her and shattered her experience into a thousand fragments almost at once. But I stayed patiently by her. I drew as a magnet draws and once again assembled all the fragments into a new order. And now already she is once again or perhaps for the first time a whole woman.'

Herself she said as much.

In a moment of the danger of excess we went out together to swim again, and she said:

'I feel whole. Oh, Louis, I am whole.'

Putting out my fingers I found her standing with hands to her breasts, head back from a throat deeply bared to the knife of the wind, and the muscles of her legs and back pulled tight as she gathered herself upward from her toes.

And I was tempted to fall on my knees upon the wet granite and say:

'Father, I praise you with my gratitude for this continual miracle, that I, with my single gift of patience, am able so to gratify and increase the loveliness of a woman beyond my understanding.'

But a moment later she was in the water and I beside her. And if I asked myself what I knew of her then I could not in honesty recount more than the powerful movement of her arms and legs across the music of the water, and the labour of her breathing apparent for a moment to ears in which blood droned and the water ran and again crowded in upon me with its own noises.

I turned and swam away from her and felt about me with slowly moving, self-hynotic limbs to find a rock. There I sat shivering and listened to the mighty suction of the water and tried to feel that it was not infinite, that facing me was land across the bay. Where she was I could not tell by any sound of her swimming, and I would not cry out to her for an answering cry because I did not wish to coerce the impassivity of things as they are, or to break with a human sound into the sufficient, ubiquitous crying of a natural tide.

She came back dripping, breathless to the rock on which I sat. And I set my hands to the delicate, strong bone of her knees and then of hips where the long muscle of her thighs disappeared, and let my fingers dwell upon the ridge of her cheek and about the sockets of her eyes, so down again to the precision of wrists and of her ankles where the she that I knew and herself claimed to be whole might seem to be least provisional and most safely held.

'Don't go away. . . .'

We turned back to Rose Gwavas and the seclusion of a room.

'Don't ever go away. . . .'

I knew that sight was only a distraction. I was not as others are tempted by last year's photographs or the sight of a face that, because it was now untouched and not quickened to immediate life, bore false witness to its own reality. My own vision was more trustworthy. A direct excitation to immediate touch gave far more certain evidence of what must be unique and dissimilar. In action and not in repose was a person truly expressed. And yet I yearned for sight. We came to a crisis upon the tide of blood and movements of the hands, and it was for me an agony of darkness. A darkness that was flooded from one moment to another with turgid, reluctant colour in its ambition to be pierced through with light and compelled to see. I desired to see the features of this head which turned with its sighs and its mumbled, crazy words from side to side upon the pillow here, although its own eyes were doubtless closed because of the excess of other sensation. I yearned for sight. If I might only once stamp the visual image like a seal upon all these single, incoherent moments that now fled away like sparks off a fire.

That moment passed, and I was content because I had in my arms a rapturously flowing woman.

Again it was a different moment, and I lay with my face in Sophie Madron's hair and her fingers loosely upon my shoulders. At an earlier moment, subsided now into memory, the same fingers had sought the small of my back, unerringly sure that from there all power and all love are born and that a man desires to feel alien, solicitous touch at the source of his love and power. Then they had fluttered like birds, lighting and taking flight again in a half panic, clutching here and there at a branch but unable to be still, pecking, clutching in the anguish of their restlessness. And were now at rest.

I thought:

'When I was eighteen I observed the phenomenon of the blurred image and wrote it down in a small note-book that a man cannot in solitude conjure up the face of his beloved, although all other faces lie in his memory perfectly lucid and clear.'

I thought:

'Sophie Madron is now the disembodied life of a pair of tempestuous hands momentarily at rest upon my shoulders. In the morning she will be herself again, and I may know what it means to have said that she is one and indivisible, a whole.'

I thought:

'It matters very little in any case. This moment is good, and so was the moment before it and the one before that.'

I awoke to hear six o'clock chiming uncertainly from the towers of Trevillian and Kingdom Come. Sophie was asleep and absolutely at peace. I did not kiss her fore-head. That would have been unchaste. I did not touch her at all but got up and went away to my own room, lay in bed there and listened to the waking birds and the jasmine rustling at my window.

The wind seemed to have changed and gone into the east to bring us rain.

I said to myself:

'Loyalty is keeping faith with that which is not itself constant. I do not know of any friendship between two

151

men which may not spoil after many years because an unexpected act on the part of one of them completely changes the other's view of him. A man is not by nature constant.'

I said:

'What it is I cherish I do not know.'

But I felt myself to be a civilised man again. I had my fill of perfection. To speak of taking the rough with the smooth was nonsense, I knew. I knew that a smooth surface was made up of a large number of imperceptibly small roughnesses.

The house was soon astir. A fire was being made in the kitchen and another in the breakfast room. I went downstairs before the breakfast was made. I went out into the garden. The wind had indeed changed into the east. It was colder. A great many older, more valetudinarian people would feel the chill of the east wind upon their stomach. I went in and ate my breakfast.

Mrs. Nance's great thighs offered resistance to my hands towards the end of her massage. Instead of that languid retirement of the pleased nerves I found an anxiety, too much feeling in the epidermis, so that the heavy limbs would not retreat from my touch nor yet allow me to coerce them into quietude.

'Something on your mind that you want to talk to me about . . .?'

Mrs. Nance said:

'Damn you, Louis. You see everything.'

And then she let me finish the job.

She dressed. And I had my cigarette, sitting on the edge of her bed.

'You make me work,' I said.

She laughed.

A pause.

Mrs. Nance said:

'Louis, I don't interfere with people's lives, do I?'

'Darling. . . .'

'I don't interfere with you, Louis, do I?'

'No.'

Another pause. Mrs. Nance got a comb and did her hair. I felt it, a page-boy's mop.

'Perfect.'

'Louis, Amity Nance is coming down the day after tomorrow. Louis . . .'

'Yes . . .?'

'Yesterday morning. Oh, I heard the two of you laughing. Sophie and you. It was a lovely sound to awake to, Louis.'

The heavy, music-hall voice had a mournful ring in it. I remembered Mrs. Nance's essential loneliness.

'Oh, Louis. You sounded both so glad to be alive. In the morning, too.'

'Yes.'

'Do you like her, Louis?'

'Yes.'

'You won't hurt her, will you? Louis . . .?'

'I shan't want to.'

'I talk too much, don't I?'

'Not to me.'

'Listen, Louis. Be discreet.'

'Because of . . .?'

'Because of Amity Nance, I suppose, though she won't hear your laughter. Her teacher . . . You know, Miss Brophy. . . . She's a pet, but she's always been rather strong on essential purity. It's not exactly that, though. It's . . . John, in a way. He knows. And he's been in a filthy sulk these last three days, Louis. You'd better watch out. I mean, I don't give a damn for the village people or anything. They think we're a bad lot, anyway. It's just the atmosphere of the house when Amity comes. She's terribly sensitive. And I'd like to have John . . . well, bearable, at least. Besides, Louis . . .'

I was a bit doubtful about whether I was being got at and how much it mattered if I were.

'. . . Sophie isn't twenty-one yet. And she's not altogether a free agent. For instance, economically. But you know all that.'

'No. I didn't know.'

'You ought to, perhaps? Oh, what the hell. It's a fact, Louis. I do talk too much. To you, I mean. The only real trouble is Amity Nance. You know how it is . . . Amity's nearly thirty, and she's terribly, terribly unspotted from the world. I blame Miss Brophy for it. But it would always be the same. Nobody can be educated by only one person, especially by a woman. And I think if Amity Nance is suddenly planted down in an atmosphere of mystery and concealed enmities it might . . . I'm damned if I know what, but something or other. Louis. . . .'

We liked each other all right.

But outside now I found the new, east wind established. Before breakfast it had been a fumbling, timid thing

154

that would have taken flight at once if the previous Atlantic wind had made up its mind to blow in again. Now
the east wind had taken possession. I got out beyond the
shelter of the house in its hollow, and a multitude of
petals from some great, sexless cherry overhead were
fluttering into my face, almost painfully cold. Rain by
to-morrow, I thought. I found the nerves under my
cheek-bones beginning to ache. It was a weather sign.
They would ache a little until the rain came and then
stop. It was a desolate moment, reminiscent of autumn,
a premature fall. This spring weather had been too
exotic to endure without a break into the summer. Prematurely hopeful plants would have their bloom wither-
ed by frost at night. Farmers would experience a melancholy pleasure at sight of the rain. I retreated again into
the shelter of the house and picked a few, clinging petals
of the cherry off the collar of my coat and out of my hair.

Part Three

*Let them alone: they be
blind leaders of the blind.
And if the blind lead the
blind, both shall fall into
the ditch. . . .*

CHAPTER NINE

I WAS UP IN my room when Amity Nance arrived. The car drew up below my window with a grinding of brakes and little stones rattling beneath the mudguards. I heard Mrs. Nance go downstairs weightily on her stick and then come out in front of the house beside the car and greet Miss Brophy with a heartiness that seemed to me a little unreal. John gave an account of the journey. Sophie came out and said good afternoon quietly and amiably, but a little breathlessly. And then there was a silence which I imagined to be an uncomfortable silence and one which nobody quite knew how to break.

They would be trying to find the most suitable way of greeting Amity Nance, wondering if they should transmit some message of welcome to her through Miss Brophy and finally giving up the problem and taking Amity Nance by the hand, Sophie shyly and with a look of inquiry at John, Mrs. Nance with an almost tearful ineptitude trying to squeeze out goodwill and sympathy through the tips of her fingers and sweat welcome at her palm. Amity Nance herself would have one hand upon Miss Brophy's hand waiting for messages to be spelt out to her, and every now and then the other hand would fly up to Miss Brophy's lips to catch at least her part in the general conversation. Amity Nance would be smiling,

smiling patiently, apologetically smiling, wanting to show that she understood and appreciated all the trouble that was being taken.

I supposed her plain. At any rate her expression, her movements would be those of a plain woman, timid and unsure, apologising for her own physical presence. Her clothes would be drab, having been chosen by another, older woman, and being worn without consciousness, without a glance down at them or a glance in the mirror. Her smile would be a dead, a dutiful smile, something learnt by touch and not a smile born of seeing other people smile from one year to another and now catching fire and reflecting pleasure caught in the eyes and lips of those around.

It was all so terribly medical, unreal and a little obscene. I became uneasy. It was a caricature of my own life and one unkindly drawn. I felt myself curiously isolated and became aware of something that I could never have properly in focus because itself was divided and unwhole.

I remembered photograph albums at home, heavy albums of thick, gilt-edged card bound in black morocco and fastened with a gold clasp, opened and pored over with a curious mixture of yearning and revulsion. It seemed to me that Amity Nance was in herself all that I had known of the awful, deathly child-woman of late Victorian days, a ghost of my own death, but even more than that a dream of my dead ancestry. I remembered the pictures, the faded, sepia lineaments of young and frightened girls dressed up in heavy skirts of serge and gaberdine, with corseted waists and masses of hair bound up about the head, pictures confused in my mind with other photographs of the same or possibly other women taken later in black, jet-ornamented bonnets, their lips stretched thin in a grin of disappointment.

It was the image of my hatred that I had conjured up as a boy on hearing some elderly, female relative say:

'When I was a girl. . . .'

I remembered being told of a picture by some contemporary artist of a young girl's body, naked, beautiful and undeveloped, with the head of an old, wrinkled beldame.

But at last the silence below my window was broken. Mrs. Nance laughed heavily, nervously, and said:

'Well. . .'

John tried to help Mrs. Nance out.

'I hope there's lots of hot tea,' said John.

'Yes, I'm sure you're all very tired and thirsty. Come along in. . . .'

And in they all went. I heard nothing but the leaves at my window rustling to the east wind. A fine drizzle lay on the wind at one moment and at another was imperceptible.

I could not bring myself to go downstairs. I lit a cigarette and stood at the window, allowing the damp air to creep over my forehead and down behind my ears, compelling the muscles of my face to relax and my mind to recapture its indifference and urbanity.

Doors opened and closed below my feet, and teathings were clinking on a tray across the hall. A conversation of sorts appeared to be slowly getting under way.

There were footsteps outside my door. Quick, delightful steps. Sophie came in, without knocking.

She said nothing. I felt the tips of her fingers alight on my shoulders and then move down to my elbows, retire and come back, settle down at my sides, and then Sophie's body was pressing up against me from behind and her hair fretting upon my ear and her knee touching the back of mine, feeling itself there and pressing in, trying to make me bend my leg.

I stood quite rigid.

'Louis, darling. Come and do your stuff.'

Sophie drew herself away from me.

'Come on, Louis.'

I did not move. I knew what would happen if I turned to Sophie just at this moment. I should turn to her for comfort. I should allow the excitement of Sophie's presence to take command of me because I was not properly in command myself, because I was a little depressed and irritated. I should be turning to Sophie in order to be soothed and calmed down.

The feelings that flickered up in me were old, dead feelings of self-pity. I thought that I had been fighting all this while without effect and that now I was to know I was defeated. I told myself that I had better take a stick and go downstairs fumbling and allow myself to be paired off with Amity Nance in a bond of common affliction and put on a gentle, ingratiating smile and allow myself to share Amity Nance's position as an object of these people's kindly interest, as an object of pity. Feelings like these flickered up in me and then one after another died down again. I despised myself for having these feelings still and had to wait until that feeling burned itself away too.

'I'll come down in just half a minute,' I said. 'You go down by yourself now.'

And as Sophie went to the door I turned round and called her back to me, to kiss her.

She had been affected by my mood. Now she laughed and went on pressing herself up against me after I had released her and refused to go away until I laughed too.

Mrs. Nance had got thoroughly into her stride now and was telling her stories of Rose Gwavas and the blood-lust retained by that great outcropping of granite outside. John was going through what I am sure were graceful evolutions with tea-cups and plates of sandwiches. Sophie's voice lay in the same direction as Mrs. Nance's, and I fancied her leaning over the back of her aunt's chair. Miss Brophy was interrupting Mrs. Nance just at that moment to inform John that Amity never had sugar in her tea and that neither did she like sweet things to eat. Mrs. Nance and Miss Brophy both broke off as I came in.

'. . And this,' said Mrs. Nance,' is Mr. Dunkel, who keeps us all in order.'

I felt Miss Brophy looming with a great push of energy before me, and then a cold, strong hand was shaking my hand in the way that is called warmly, and the voice that I immediately characterised as defiant had cast off its quality of defiance and taken on the tones of proprietary interest. I squirmed inwardly at the woman, but could not help at the same time feeling that Miss Brophy was in all probability an extremely interesting and often a highly admirable person and at any rate impressive.

'. . . And this,' said Miss Brophy, 'is Amity, my little pupil.'

She went to fetch Amity Nance to me. There was a pause, during which I suppose my name and I thought some instruction on what to say to me were spelt into Amity Nance's hand. And then a hand, very hot and moist, trembling a little, had found its way to mine and was making signs which I found I had lost the habit of reading quickly and without effort, but which conveyed to me vague, trite messages to the effect that Amity Nance had been told I was as she was, blind, and that she was happy to meet me because she knew that I was a very distinguished, good man, and how pleasant it was to come to the house of these beautiful people who took so much trouble to be kind to poor, blind people like ourselves.

I shivered.

My first impulse was one of pity. I could not bear that any woman should have been brought up to such triteness of thought. I hated Miss Brophy. It was as if she had compelled her pupil's mind to remain that of a child in order to keep ascendancy over it or even for a moment as if she had taught Amity this ludicrous, inept language for the sole purpose of holding her up to ridicule. And then I recoiled from what I found hideous. A bully, a liar, or a sexually infantile person is not less hateful because one understands that all his failures in conformity are due in the last resort to the folly and incomprehension of his upbringing. And I could not help being

164

oppressed by what struck me as hopeless, unmitigable ugliness in Amity Nance.

Another pause. The one hand remained lightly resting against mine, piteously sweating with its anxiety, while the other I fancied flew up to Miss Brophy's lips and down to her fingers and up again, piteously anxious to let nothing slip by.

Miss Brophy said:

'You could speak ordinarily to her if you found it easier, Mr. Dunkel.'

And the fingers were transferred from Miss Brophy's lips to my own.

I realised that I must coerce myself into a state of mind sufficiently amiable to allow some kind of socially possible response. I accepted the rôle of very distinguished, good man and muttered something fatherly and encouraging. I don't remember what it was.

Miss Brophy shepherded Amity back to her chair and herself remained standing. Mrs. Nance was conscious of my, at any rate, possible embarrassment and boomed out with extreme heartiness that my chair had been put next to Amity's. Miss Brophy was evidently for helping me across the room. I heard her bend down and remove some piece of crockery that was two or three feet out of my path. Sophie and John had been silent all this while. I made my way with exaggerated lack of difficulty to the empty chair over on the other side of the fireplace. Miss Brophy sat down. John gave me tea. I felt that he was at the moment completely sympathetic. Mrs. Nance took up the conversation where she had left it.

'. . . I was telling that one about the dog, Louis.'

'Oh, yes.'

'I'm sure it's not suitable for Amity, but Miss Brophy might like it. . . .'

A dig at Miss Brophy, I thought. I applauded it, unconscious though it no doubt was.

'Yes. . . .'

Mrs. Nance went on.

It was one of the whole string of Rose Gwavas stories testifying to the blood-lust of Rose Gwavas heath. An old, avaricious woman of the Madron ancestry had lived at Rose Gwavas five generations back with her son. Lived when she ought to have died, that is to say. She had lain year after year in her bed and refused either to die or to give her son a single penny of her money while she lived. After one of an apparently unending series of quarrels that always began with a request for money, the son had finished up as often before by swearing that he would go straight down and hang himself if the old woman still refused. As before she had refused him so much as a penny. He had gone downstairs in his violence, swearing to find her money and steal it, swearing that he would hang himself, swearing to burn the house down over her head. And then a bright idea. . . . Perhaps it had started with a mere rage to destroy something, anything. At any rate this young man, a Madron ancestor, had hoisted up a noose to one of the beams in the hall, and then he had dragged and coaxed a great deerhound on to a table placed under the noose and had got the noose about the animal's neck and then had kicked the table away and stood beside the struggling, shrieking animal, half mad with pleasure. As the table fell and the great dog entered into its agony of death the old woman upstairs had experienced one last pang of motherly concern.

'He's done it. He swore he would, and now he's gone and hanged himself at last.'

Struggling out of bed she had reached the top of the stairs, staggered, collapsed and fallen headlong, broken her neck. And a week or two afterwards her son had inherited all her money and found that he did not know what to do with it any more than she.

Mrs. Nance told the story beautifully. The Cornish talk that she used was a stage Cornish, richer and more rare than anything to be heard in the villages at that late day, but she made it altogether convincing and satisfying. Miss Brophy did not like the story. She laughed and said that she was afraid Amity would not really appreciate it. Amity made no audible sign, and there was no pause. I gathered she had been trained to know when a conversation was outside Miss Brophy's taste in what was suitable for her. I wondered how much of Miss Brophy's life-long care of Amity was spontaneously actuated by love of however misguided a variety, and how much by desire for a rôle of high moral prestige which people of lofty principles would applaud in her. John laughed dutifully at his aunt's story and adjusted some error in the minor detail of her telling of it. A curious, forced giggle came from Sophie, and I hated it and then told myself that I was not the only person in the room sensitive enough to feel embarrassment of one kind or another.

I told myself that I was being excessively self-conscious and therefore stupid. It was neurotic to find in Amity Nance a reflection of myself and to suffer personally from what I felt about her existence. There was more difference between Amity Nance and myself than there is between an emotionally retarded and a highly sophisticated person among those who do see with their eyes. To recoil from her in self-pity was as if a man with red hair should begin to hate himself because he had been to some court of law and seen a red-haired criminal. It was neurotic, and that was all there was to it.

But I was disturbed. I was troubled by my sense of the ugliness of it all, and the ugliness was of that kind which is common to all freakish and abortive things, to the five-legged animal in a show-case and to the idiot, to the dwarf and the giant, to the mutilated legless man, the double-yolked egg and the rooster that changes its sex, to the peppered beams, the timbering of suburban architecture, the transvestiture of the Christmas pantomime with its plump-thighed, sweet and pigeon-breasted hero and his male, bewigged mother with her muscular legs and derisive voice and to the unused sink, concealed behind a Japanese screen, to all unnatural death and monstrous birth. All things are good except insofar as they are denatured. And I had died at least the premature, unnatural death of my eyes. I was in my own degree abortive and a freak. I could not help finding a partial image of myself in whatever I might feel about Amity Nance. And I was disturbed above all by the pity that would every now and then leap up in me like a salmon leaping in the stream, and by the necessity for my own comfort of stifling that feeling and refusing it play.

I went into Sophie's room. Amity Nance had gone to bed an hour ago. Miss Brophy had followed. The two of them were housed in rooms next to each other at a corner of the house farthest away from Sophie's room. Mrs. Nance and John were still downstairs talking no doubt about household diplomacies and what to do with Amity on the following day.

Sophie was in bed. I felt the heat from a little radiator let into the wall and heard its occasional buzzing. The light, I fancied, was on, a hard, electric blaze, and Sophie was waiting in bed for me, a little keyed up and a little restless.

I went to her room in a mood I could only describe as one of inquiry, inquiry of a vague, directionless kind which did not know to what question it sought an answer. Amity Nance was present in the house, insistent. It was impossible to function as if she were not there. She was like some obstreperous, late guest who, now having got here, refused to behave according to the rules of the house. It was everybody's problem. Her very quietness was as disturbing as the presence of a pacifist at a dinner of hunting, shooting and fishing gentlemen or as the presence of Colonel Blimp at a week-end gathering of left-wing intellectuals or on Friday night at a working men's club. It was impossible to function normally as though she were not there, impossible to ignore her, and certainly it was difficult to acknowledge her presence and adjust one's faculties to it. A mood of inquiry prevailed, but the questions refused to formulate themselves in answerable terms.

For me the mood was aggravated by a sense of the

169

falsity of my own position. In my own, similar way I also must have been everybody's problem little more than a couple of weeks ago, though I flattered myself that I had a talent for becoming quickly inconspicuous. And yet I was inclined to ally myself with Rose Gwavas, with the normal, seeing people, against the intruder. It turned me into a creature left stranded between two worlds to neither of which I belonged, and I suffered from my sense of isolation. Again I had the sensation of being a stranded merman. Only now I had put on a lounge suit, professed Christian principles and found myself joining people of the dry land in shooting their nets. So must a man feel in a civil war who finds himself living happily on what he knows to be the wrong side of the barricades, unable for personal as well as military reasons to cross the battle-front and rejoin his true companions. In such a way, too, have I often thought of the working-class boys I used to play with in the streets of Norwich and who would not see my face now for my clothes, but would peer indifferently through from the public bar into the saloon where the beer was charged a halfpenny more and who, if they thought I claimed at heart to be one of them, would shrug their shoulders and think it so much the worse for me.

Out of pure self-protection I had to falsify my thought.

I went and sat on the edge of Sophie's bed. She brought out one arm, slight and cool, from among the bed clothes and put a hand somewhere uncertainly to rest upon my knee.

She stayed a moment thus without any other movement, and I fancied her smiling up at me with a radiance

of troubled gladness in my being with her, because when
at last she spoke her voice was heavily charged and eager
to be heard and to obtain a response.

'Louis . . .'

I delayed my response.

Sophie did not want to talk either about Amity Nance
or about anything else. I admired her essential wisdom
even then. She was troubled as I was, at any rate because
I was. And from that point there was a gap between us.
I wanted to settle with the trouble and put all the untroubled rightness between us into abeyance until the
trouble was settled with. Sophie wanted to put the
trouble in abeyance until to-morrow and in the meantime let the untroubled rightness of love establish itself
more completely between us. I admired the more whole-
some impulse of her quiet, perfectly sound womanhood,
but I was not able to accept it. I had to mention Amity
Nance, and when I did so it jolted her poise of feeling,
though I do not think she knew it.

'It's all so ugly,' I said.

And Sophie withdrew the hand from my knee and
let it lie upon the counterpane.

She made the necessary adjustment of her feeling and
sighed.

'It's terribly sad,' she said.

And then breathed in and for a moment held her
breath as if in doubt whether that were the truly appropriate thing she had meant to say.

But again she did not want to talk or even to think.
She lay quite still and waited for me to have finished
wanting to talk.

I did my own bit of sighing.

'Ugly, ugly,' I said, 'and only sad because of the ugliness.'

And I turned to Sophie and put my hands under her shoulders and my face down in her hair. The desire awakened in me, flickered through my veins and made my breathing difficult. I have never found any woman whose power to excite lay so readily on the surface as it did with Sophie Madron. At a few seconds of contact her cheek was so hot it almost burned into me with the wonderful, dry heat of blood coming responsively to the surface in touch.

But I turned away from her.

I must not offer myself to Sophie with a trouble in my mind. The relationship between us could stand a good deal by now. It had reached that stage of ease in which the deftnesses of love, the little perversities of the court-esan were able to be indulged with perfect freedom. The first solemnity, that perilous solemnity of a woman fal-ling in love which on every occasion had to be carefully, painstakingly wooed away, had subsided. A delicate har-lotry was in play, a honey-getting, butterfly affair. We had come into that purely delightful, intermediate phase between the conclusion of a courtship and the beginning of matedness, the space of fair, untroubled weather in the middle of a cyclone in which pleasure may safely be cultivated for its own sake. And at the same time there was at any rate that degree of closeness, of bondage and tenacity, between us that if we had been separated for a week we should both have suffered profoundly, and on meeting again should have rushed together like soul and body amid the flames of an opening grave in William Blake's engraving. It was like that. Nevertheless there were still buds and leaves to be coaxed with the utmost gentleness into unfolding, still a reluctant tendril here and there, a kind of chastity, a reserve, which made it imperative that love should not yet be made cheaply, that a certain vigilance should not yet be relaxed, in case some unguarded impulse of the mind in loving inexpensively, without cost (for costliness is a guarantee), should reveal itself to be in fact a canker. And so I would not stay with Sophie in to-night's mood.

Her arms were about my neck, and she wanted to be pulled up with me, the weight of her body barely sufficient to afflict a man with languor. I disengaged her arms with all the courtesy that such an ungracious act is susceptible of, and she lay back unquiet and full of half-resentful awakedness, the breath weightily balanced upon her parted lips.

I bent to kiss her and thought of the other first occasion on which I had left her lying thus unassuaged, and marvelled at what a strength of passion had grown up in her since then, although even then passion had seemed to me to be strong in her.

At the door I halted. Mrs. Nance and John were just coming upstairs, and I thought it better to wait here until they had gone into their rooms. I did not speak, and neither did Sophie speak to me.

But at six o'clock in the morning she came into my room. I awoke to hear the door opening and bare feet coming towards me over the varnished wood and the

173

moment after deadened by a rug, and then Sophie was climbing into my bed with crumpled silk upon a body already a little chilled from morning air which invaded the landings of the house.

She lay close up against me, but did not put her arms about me or compel my arms to go about her. A moment she lay in silence, inclined to shiver at first, while I awakened more completely and became aware of the sleepy, first chittering of sparrows at the window, and then she started talking in a voice that was half assumed cheerfulness and half the earnestness of explaining things of which the mind was not yet altogether sure.

'I didn't sleep a wink. . . .'

And I understood how she had lain in bed trying to discover the magic formula that would set my mind at rest about Amity Nance.

'. . . When you say it's ugly, Louis, I . . . well, I've been trying to understand what you meant, what you're feeling about it. As a matter of fact, Amity's extremely pretty, herself. Only, of course, you weren't to know that. And what you call ugly . . . well, I think I know what you meant now, but it isn't there at all. Really, Louis . . .'

I had never heard Sophie talk so much except on the afternoon when she had taken me up to Chy Tralee. The words tumbled out. I laughed at her.

'. . . No, listen. I said it was sad, and you said it was only sad because it was ugly. As a matter of fact, it's sad because it's brave, Louis. And it's brave and sad because it's beautiful. That's something you can't tell just now, though you will in time. I wish you could see her, Louis. Amity's really pretty, and she's so patient and tranquil and . . . well, I suppose I mean womanly. Louis . . .'

She drew herself more tightly against me, and I put my arms about her.

'. . . Honestly, she is. . . .'

I laughed. But it was a laugh of restraint.

'. . . Louis, listen. . . .'

Sophie was absolutely grave now. At first she had been embarrassed at saying so much, at appearing as a talkative woman, nagging at me, taking the initiative, and at the possibility of being laughed at.

'. . . Listen, Louis. Do you know what your face was like yesterday? It was tightened up, closed up, and all the life had gone out of it. Do you know how full of life your face is? It's like a hare's face when it's listening in the middle of a field, like a hunting cat's face, sensitive and alight. Do you know how much more alive you seem than other people? It's as if they took the world for granted because they can see it while you're always poised and quiet, listening, waiting and as sensitive . . . sensitive as a . . .'

'. . . Woman?'

'No, listen. I'm serious. It's difficult. I can't think what the most sensitive things are. Trees, perhaps. A tree in autumn, a young ash tree in spring, the moonlight sometimes. I don't know. And all of a sudden comes Amity, and it faded out of you and left you looking dull and resentful. I think it's because you turned in suddenly upon yourself. And you mustn't. Amity's a person, a lovely thing. And you must be aware of her like that. I think you're only being aware of yourself. She makes you turn in upon yourself, and then you've lost everything. Louis . . . .'

Sophie was trembling with the effort of discovering what she really meant, and she was excited. Her fingers moved about my face, loving me. I did not want to laugh any more. I felt curiously bleak. The waking birds outside were timid of the weather. Only Sophie's feet at the bottom of the bed were an everlasting comfort. I thought the rain would settle in.

'. . . All tense, like an ordinary man. Like Trevor Beed or John. . . .'

Sophie's voice was confident and hushed now.

'. . . You'll have to get those wonderful, powerful hands of yours to work on yourself. Make yourself stop frowning, Louis. Do you know what power of healing there is in your hands?'

'They're guided from the head. When the head's confused, there's no virtue in the hands.'

'Forget your head, Louis. Be nice to Amity. Forget yourself. Don't curl up like a snail in its shell. There's nothing to hurt. Louis, I do love you. I do. Does Auntie know . . .?'

'Know . . .?'

'. . . About us? I know John does. He scowls at me wherever I go. I should think he's probably scowling now. But does Auntie know?'

'Yes, she knows. She says I'm not to hurt you.'

'She is a sweet thing, isn't she? I won't be hurt, don't you worry. But what I meant is if Auntie knows I'm going to stay here until we get up.'

'Auntie said I had to be discreet.'

'Yes, but not me.'

'She'd expect me to throw you out if you were difficult.'

'But you won't, will you? And I'm not. I only want to be warm. I only. . . . Oh, Louis, I do love you. I do. . . .'

CHAPTER TEN

MEMORY IS IN one sense or another the clue to all things. It is the continuum, the ambience in which all our disjointed moments cohere into a whole. And it is certainly not what the common use of language would lead us to suppose. It is not for instance a specific faculty of the mind with which we go fishing into the past, angling for some incident or other which takes the bait or eludes it in the same apparently capricious way as ordinary fishes do. No, it is all-pervading. It is the all-pervading activity of life, the principle of human existence, and if we began to understand it we should be a great deal nearer than we are to knowledge of the world in which we live.

At present we are beginning to understand not memory itself but certain kinds of failure in memory.

Dr. Freud lectured to his students in Vienna and told them that if we forgot some episode in our own lives, or a word or face associated with it, that was because our mind rejected it as something disturbing to us and therefore undesirable. Dr. Freud told his students also that if we forgot some possession of ours and left it behind at a friend's house, or in the train, that showed either that we wished to lose it or that we wanted an excuse for returning at least in phantasy to the place in which it had been left. These observations of that great Jewish doctor are, I believe, just and penetrating, but they tell us nothing about memory. They tell us something about the private meaning of our own lapses of memory, or as I would prefer to call them our own lapses from memory. For memory is there all the time, and it is we who lapse from it as a man lapses from his religion, and it is precisely into this private meaning that we do lapse, for there is nothing private about memory, but only about forgetfulness.

I have an extremely good memory. It is necessary that I should have, because I have fewer means of maintaining the continuity of my life from one day to the next than people have whose eyes recognise for them what has been seen before and warn the mind continually of the strange, the new and the incomprehensible wherever it may present itself. In a very definite sense I believe that good memory is a guarantee of my integrity, my own singleness of life. At any rate, when I forget something or when my remembrance of something is vague and blurred, I begin to worry and realise that at that point occurred a failure in living, a confusion of purpose, an evasion of whatever issue it was that I now try without success to conjure up again in all its detail.

Up to the time of Amity Nance's arrival every day and almost every hour of my stay at Rose Gwavas survives in my mind with a high degree of clarity, if I except the two or three days of Sophie's first retirement before she committed herself in any way to me. But after Amity Nance's arrival the days tend to run into each other. As I search about in memory for this or that particular incident and mood I find myself running into banks of mist, and occasionally into total oblivion, just as if the east wind at that time had saturated my mind, too, with the sea-fret.

I should like to understand this completely. But if I did I should understand myself completely. And if that were possible my understanding of all things would be complete.

Besides, if I understood I should remember again, and so there would be nothing to understand.

As it is I understand in part. And I find that when some effort of mind enables me to understand a little better the weather lifts in more places than one and I also remember a little better.

We do not remember pain. This is a commonplace by now. There is no memory of pain. And the reason for this, as it seems to me, is that pain is outside our life, is alien to it, is a partial death and therefore a simple negation of life or a lapse from it. I have no doubt that a sick man remembers his pain so long as he remains sick, and it is possible that the dead are aware of death if awareness of a negative is possible. But a healthy man does not remember pain, and a man back from the edge of the grave cannot recollect anything of his death. If we try to look back on these things we see ourselves remotely and ineffectually as a stranger is seen. We remember that we gnawed the pillow or bit our own hands with pain because that was vital action, the action of a healthy body resisting its pain, but the pain itself is out of us, a fragment of deathliness that we cast out, and we regard our own strange, writhing movements now with-

180

out comprehension. They not only seem, but they are the contortions of a stranger.

It is the same with confusion of mind from which we have truly emerged and with guilt from which we are now absolved. They were interruptions, falsifications of our life, assailing us from without, compelling us to a private, imprisoned life, and now we can only stand apart and look back wonderingly upon the words, thoughts, deeds, wishes and prayers they forced out of us at the time.

I look back upon the very brief period of Amity Nance's presence in my life, and I see the mist clearing in patches, lifting on a breeze and closing in again, here and there shot through with a ray of light unusually clear, in other places full of the most eerie phantasies of light. These patches of illumination represent the good, the living moments. The rest is, I feel, permanently obscured for me by the confusion, the falsity of mind which held me back from normal contact with reality at the moment. And the period most obstinately shrouded in mist is composed of the few days as it seems, but it may have been two or three weeks, between the day after Amity's arrival and the moment at which I presently realised that a fight of some kind was on and I'd better watch out.

During that period I was clenched hard against Amity Nance's reality. I spent a good deal of time with her, and even more time numbing myself against her, but I would not allow the reality of her presence to impinge upon me. I was treating her as an institution, talking with her as a duty, as if I were giving her private tuition in the elements of a subject of which I was master and only doing so for the sake of earning a livelihood.

But here and there the reality began to penetrate my defences, and those penetrations are the moments that I do remember.

For instance, the moment at which Amity quite unexpectedly spelled into my hand the words:

'I think we ought to stop for to-day. You've been frowning so much, and your hands are so listless, I feel sure you're too worried to be bothered with me. I talk so much.'

How stupid I had been. It had not dawned on me how subtle her touch was, and that all this while that our hands had been rapidly spelling out a conversation the edge of her little finger-nail had been exploring deeper into my palm, or that while I was talking aloud, and she reading the movements of my lips, she had also been examining the structure and the mood expressed in the muscles of my face, and that in the space of a few days she had probably learnt a hundred times more about me than I about her. I felt as if I had been set guessing by a child of five, and then I had a feeling of relief because I understood that reality and liveliness of some kind Amity Nance undoubtedly had and I was a fool to ignore it.

I suddenly realised, too, that although one organ did service for both, the language of her fingers, as she used the manual alphabet, was pure social tittle-tattle, that the exploration was infinitely more real for her and that the language she used for purposes of true self-expression had not yet come into being. I had been revolted by the triteness of her language, the everlasting use of words like 'beautiful,' 'kind,' 'good,' and what I took to be the corresponding triteness and falsity of her receptiveness to experience. Now I wondered. It must be that she had a darker, more vivid awareness, too, for which Miss Brophy had not catered.

But I at once thought:

'Her sense of touch is infinitely more delicate than Sophie's, and Sophie's fingers are not inept.'

I compared. And that was bad. It robbed the moment of its worth.

And it was strange. I did not even discover what things I hated about Amity Nance until the moment at which I discovered that I did not hate them after all.

One of these things was her personal cleanliness.

It came from Miss Brophy. And Miss Brophy was a woman without coquetry. I do not know what soap she got for Amity when they were in Falmouth. Carbolic, I should think, or at best some pure, unscented oatmeal. And Amity Nance had that kind of feel about her, and I hated it. I found it obscene. Powder, rouge, liquid scent, scented shampoos were things that Amity had not been introduced to. She smelled clean as a little girl or an old, dry woman smells clean, and her clothes matched the smell, being prim and without interest either to herself or to anybody else, and therefore in a woman of just under thirty unnatural. I hated these things, and I did not know I was hating them. I thought it was Amity herself who repelled me.

I remember that for a few minutes one afternoon just before tea the drizzle stopped, and the sun came out.

Amity was quickly aware of the fact. Like a very sensitive barometer, I thought.

I made upon her fingers the words:

'Perhaps you would like to go out into the garden now.'

I did not care very much whether she would like to go out into the garden or not. I wanted to go out into the garden. It was oppressive to sit here tutoring *The New Beacon's* delight in one or another of the dismal, elementary sub-divisions of human knowledge, pretending all the while that it was intimate conversation.

The sodden earth began to steam under the sun and yield up all its delicious, pent-up odours. It pleased and refreshed me. Amity was enraptured. I heard her breathing deeply, lingeringly, and her movements quickened. The fingers with which she preserved her contact with me became excited. She was alive. And for the moment her presence lost its oppressiveness for me.

My nostrils selected and chose among the many odours, the earth itself and a late hyacinth. And I was baffled for a moment by the absence of the odour I thought of as woman beside me and realised then that I had become so used to cosmetics that their odour was the one which had received the name of presence of woman in my mind.

I thought:

'Cosmetics are used to excite men whose nostrils are dulled, and here am I unable to tolerate the presence of a woman without that sign of her womanhood flaunted before me. Yet I am one who regarded himself as in all senses but one immeasurably superior to ordinary men.'

And I was tempted to rejoice in Amity Nance's presence, but stifled the temptation.

I came alive, I think, the day on which she opened her mouth and spoke.

As if to provoke that effect I had just allowed my fingers to travel over her face and down upon her shoulders and arms.

I knew that with her infinitely light, flying fingers she had already taken the cast of my features. I must, in my clumsier way, do the same by her. Not because I wanted to know her. I would have preferred to remain completely aloof. But it was something expected of me by Sophie, something expected of me by Mrs. Nance and something whose continued absence left me at a disadvantage. Sophie had enjoined it. And I knew that Sophie at least was right.

How easily the feelings appropriate to adolescence recapture the mind as soon as it becomes self-engrossed.

For half an hour I had sat beside Amity Nance speculating whether I could permit myself to examine her face or not. I was like a boy of seventeen wondering how best to start things with a girl, what her response would be to an arm about her waist, whether then the attempt to kiss would result in a smacked face, and whether after that a more intimate caress would call forth tears, indignation, a quiet, firm refusal or the blossoming forth of passion which might be more embarrassing still than any of these. And then I had put the tips of my fingers to Amity Nance's temples and let them move into a clear, open forehead and down over deep cheek-bones and bridges of the straight nose to a friendly, thin-lipped

mouth, one without tautness, without any development
of muscle about it, and to a chin smoothly developed, not
in the least hard, yet giving squareness rather than oval-
ness to the whole face. It was a face that I liked. Nothing
was too deeply bitten into it, neither pain nor effort. I
approved of it. And then, as imperceptibly as I might
and fearful lest she might take it for a caress, I had let
my fingers slip down over throat and shoulders and the
tips just barely pass her breasts to know what depth and
heaviness of a woman she was.

It was not a caress. There was no hint of sexual exploration in it. I was attempting simply to receive the
impression of a person whom it was imperative that I
should know. And the movement had been taken as it
was intended, naturally, as if sitting still to have a photograph taken, a necessity as between people who could
not see each other.

Whatever other harm she might have done to her
pupil Miss Brophy had evidently not kept on telling her:
'Beware of wicked men.'

Or at any rate if she had Amity had not listened to her.

But I think the contact must have stirred up something in her all the same.

She opened her mouth and spoke.

I wish it were possible to reproduce the effect of her
voice.

Evidently she had learnt to speak by feeling the movements of other people's and especially of Miss Brophy's
lips and tongue, but she had never heard words spoken.
When she herself spoke she had no means of knowing
what it sounded like. She could only form her lips and

tongue into the shapes that she had learnt and then speak out into a void and ask Miss Brophy to correct her.

The result as I heard it now was extraordinary.

It was a speech more foreign than that of any foreigner speaking the unfamiliar tongue. It had not even the naturel focus of a voice. It was curiously ventriloquial, coming as if not from Amity Nance's mouth at all. It was loud, and it was toneless, brutish. And yet there was the vibration of humanity in it. The words were nothing.

She said, as she had said with her fingers on our first meeting:

'You are as I am, blind.'

But the words came out of such a depth of unconsciousness, a wild, animal cry resounding from the infinite past or a god speaking brutishly through a woman.

I trembled, and I dare say I wanted to cry.

For the first time that night I went on thinking about Amity Nance after I had left her. Her voice kept breaking tonelessly, monstrously into my sleep.

Could it be that this child of thirty excited me? I would not allow myself so much as the supposition. After waking and dozing with the sound of her voice in my ears time and again until three o'clock in the morning, the rain dripping incessantly outside my window, I got up and went back to Sophie's room and stayed there and presently slept.

Before breakfast on what must, I fancy, have been the second or third Sunday after their arrival, but it may have been the first, Miss Brophy set everybody running

187

about, telephoning and getting out the car, to find out
where the nearest Catholic church was and at what time
High Mass could be heard. It was characteristic of the
woman's personal firmness that she had not wasted our
time or her own with previous intimations that she
might be wanting a church or something of the kind
come Sunday. I doubt whether it had even been gathered
that Miss Brophy was a practising Catholic at all, or
Mrs. Nance would have made provision. Now everybody
tried to be helpful, and nobody knew anything to the
point. Mrs. Nance rang up nonconformist and Anglican
parsons whose names she knew, but all were in bed or
out of the house except the old, suspicious Baptist minister
who pretended he did not know the whereabouts of the
enemy's position. Eventually John drove out to ask the
Beeds, des Voeux and such of the neighbourhood as
were not on the telephone and discovered contrary to all
hope that Major des Voeux, who was already at his
tomatoes, knew both time and place, though he also
made the pretence of having forgotten at first.

I came downstairs just as John returned with the car,
leaving it outside to be ready in the drive. For the first
time since I had arrived at Rose Gwavas we all had
breakfast together. Everybody was excited, but Sophie
began to withdraw herself from the excitement of the
others as soon as I was established at the table.

Miss Brophy was saying:

'. . . But I didn't take her as far as confirmation. I'm
afraid Amity can't be made to understand sin.'

That, too, was characteristic of the woman, and I applauded it. Amity had probably been baptised by her

188

parents in another faith. Miss Brophy had given her as much Catholic religious teaching as seemed reasonable, had even gone so far as to get a priest in to help her through the Penny Catechism. But when she saw that Amity's understanding and experience did not cover certain of the Christian essentials she had stopped the whole business at that point—neither despairing of her pupil's soul nor of her own teachers, simply accepting the matter as it stood. I imagine it had not even been a great disappointment to her. What she felt about Amity's spiritual condition I cannot imagine. Herself reasonably devout and doctrinally quite sound she must have felt that Amity unconfirmed was not a particularly safe investment in the life to come. The spiritual gulf between her pupil and herself must have been apparent to her. But like many good Catholics she managed to keep different matters in different, insulated compartments, and the relationship between the two remained unaltered. Meantime Amity was taken to Mass every other Sunday or so and no doubt received a signal from Miss Brophy when to kneel and when to stand and certainly smelled the growing cloud of incense and may even have felt a vibration in the bell's excitement.

But reflection on this matter was broken off by the fact that the tone of John's voice had suddenly become interesting.

Mrs. Nance said:

And what are you going to do, John?'

John rose at it immediately as if somebody were trying to cheat him of his rights.

'Going to do?'

'Yes, John dear. You'll have to find something to do with yourself while Mass is on. You can't just sit in the car and snore outside the church. I mean to say . . .'

John tried to sound as if he were just being thoroughly tactful.

'Oh, I shall go to Mass, too. I shall love to,' he said.

Mrs. Nance was, I fancy, conscious of his feeling and inclined to probe it.

'I'm sure Miss Brophy doesn't insist on that. Do you now? What I was thinking was that perhaps Louis might go in with you, and then the two of you could drive round and have a boyish chat until the service is over.'

'Well, of course, if—er—Louis. . . .'

'No, no.'

I put in my protest. Poor John was thoroughly confused. He was dying to go to Mass with Amity and Miss Brophy and very anxious that we shouldn't know it, but I fancy becoming aware that we did.

'No, really,' he said. 'I should love to go to Mass.'

And laughed a little so that we could still believe that he was simply being thoughtful, if we cared to.

Mrs. Nance gave him a last dig.

'Perhaps Louis would like to go Mass, then?'

'Oh, no,' I said. 'It isn't tennis. Or bridge. You don't have to make up the four. And I feel very little need of absolution at the moment.'

And that was that. People began to disappear from the breakfast table, and I do not think that anybody else went on pondering over John's anxiety to go to Mass. But John went on being anxious, fussing about with rugs and things and keeping a close watch on the time, and

I felt that at any rate he had entered into a definite alliance with Amity and Miss Brophy against the rest of us, with Amity against the world or with Miss Brophy against his aunt.

I remember that little episode very well, and I remember that after it Sophie and I went for a Sunday morning walk. I think we went up to Chy Tralee, but I am not certain of that. Sophie, I remember, was properly dressed for a Sunday morning walk. She had on a costume of light tweed, a flopping hat with a feather and shoes that sucked at the earth as if they were soled with crêpe rubber. She carried a stick, too. The rain was only intermittent by that time and seemed to be leaving us.

We talked about our respective feelings for the Catholic Church. Its voluptuousness had, I think, appealed greatly to Sophie at one time or another, though now she was inclined to hate it more than anything for its reactionary politics and its indifference to human suffering. I said that for myself I could imagine accepting all the doctrine, but that if I did so that of itself would prevent me from becoming a practising Catholic. If I really believed that those little wafers served at Mass, with the light shining through them and making them look shiny, were indeed the body of Christ, then I should be afraid of ever bringing myself to eat them because I should expect them to wriggle as they grew hot on my tongue. I thought that practising Catholics who really believed must be either terribly brave or terribly insensitive. But perhaps that clamorous and insistent ringing of the bell as a Mass approached its most solemn moment only exalted and encouraged them, whereas it terrified me and made me feel that if I did not get up at once and go out into the open air I should lose consciousness.

I also said that I thought Amity had a little of the holy relic about her, that her particular odour was definitely the odour of sanctity and that I should similarly expect her to wriggle on the tongue. This worried Sophie, and she worked very hard to explain to me what Amity was really like.

From this point the story might perfectly well proceed at its former pace. The only thing is that if I allowed it to do so either I should have to cover dozens of pages with my own private reflections or I should have to make a violent effort of the imagination to present all that happened from somebody else's point of view.

John's, for instance.

For although I remember almost every minute of my time with the clarity called 'as if it were yesterday' I was in fact living inwardly, feeding myself on phantasies, to such a degree that when I presently woke up I found that I had got left behind by my own action and that the other actors in my story were so far ahead of me that it had already ceased to be my story in any but a purely technical sense.

In addition to which there is much that was at the time painful and still is incompletely annealed and which I would be glad enough to be allowed, without the thought that I was in some way cheating my reader, to pass over in silence.

A diary of events with the dates as nearly exact as I can make them would record the following.

May 30. Miss Brophy's departure.
She went to stay with her relatives in Connaught.

I fancy that Miss Brophy's departure was engineered by Mrs. Nance from her studio upstairs. It was the first time in fourteen years that Miss Brophy had allowed herself to be separated from her pupil. Mrs. Nance must have worked quite hard to convince her that it was a possible and even a desirable thing to do, and she had worked, I fancy, first in the interests of Amity's liberation of mind and second because she thought Miss Brophy's presence irked me, as indeed it did, though I admired the woman very much.

June 2-3. The first occasion on which I might consciously have wished Sophie Madron to be other or elsewhere than she was.

I remember this occasion very well. It was I suppose in essence a mere, self-correcting disease of proximity such as must be almost chronic in the lives of married people. I withdrew myself and for the first time contemplated Sophie objectively. It did not matter that I found her beautiful, as I most certainly and heart-breakingly did. She had just that slenderness and tautness of body which can never settle into banality. Every inch of her lived with its own life because she had a natural, voluptuous pleasure in the most insignificant movement of her own limbs. In the very lowest estimate she must always be a piece of mobile, living sculpture of which a man could never tire. But all that mattered in **that** moment was **that** I became terribly clear-headed and critical, and sudden clear-headedness I have always found to be the outward and perceptible sign of confused emotions, of emotions that have suddenly made contact and engaged in battle down in the subterranean places.

I began to watch Sophie for signs that she was not so perfect in herself as she ought to have been.

At heart I believe I wanted her to awake and say something utterly stupid in order that I might quarrel with her mind.

I waited for her to open her mouth and snore. And if she had snored I should have wanted to strangle her.

She had a life apart from me. I wanted to come into her closer, to destroy the last atom of separateness. And I knew what that meant. It meant that in a moment I should be wanting to strike her, to make her cry out and gape at me with pain, because there is no other way.

I lay beside her and felt that I should suffocate, so that I might have the excuse to clutch, to tear.

And then I turned my thoughs away from her, as if that were the most insidious cruelty of all.

I thought of Amity:

'Amity Nance has no past, and therefore her life is without separateness. It is not in her power to make another person lonely. Her life is continuous, from the day of her birth until a day far beyond to-morrow. Thirty years have gone by in a continuous effort to know the world about her, and there has been no break of any kind, no sudden weariness or sense of loss to clot the flow of her emotion as blood clots. Her life is continuous, and her innocence is absolute. She has no past. Her life has never doubled back upon itself or fled away round irretraceable corners like a fugitive thief wandering perpetually about his mother's house where he knows the police are waiting for him. And her life has never been anything but trustful, has never broken faith. From the first moment she had to trust other people not to lead her astray, trust the earth she could not see to sustain her feet. And her innocence is absolute because she has never known anxiety or fear and never turned her back on whatever presented itself to her. She has grown patiently and humbly towards the present moment, and it is with flawless patience and humility that she will suffer whatever is to follow.'

I thought thus of Amity Nance and in the same instant turned to Sophie Madron, sleeping quietly and without a doubt happily beside me. I put my mouth to the loved, high ridge of her cheek where the night air lay cool and the strong hair coiled at my lip. I wanted to rouse her, but did not. I let my hands outside the bed-clothes flow down the length of her to the feet which lay together like hands clasped in surprise or wrung with anguish, and then I got up and went away to my own room.

8 June. What a reasonable neurologist would diagnose as emotional fatigue, a theologian as accidia and a French novelist as *une crise de nerfs*. Myself I called it stalemate.

All morning I played the piano. I played myself dizzy, and I played viciously, trying to make music that would

195

keep everybody else out of the music-room. I was in terror lest Mrs. Nance should come to sit in the room listening to me, and I played to keep her away. I had not wanted to give her the massage this morning. I had cultivated phantasies, fancying that perhaps Sophie would come to me in the kind of purity of mind with which she had wrapped herself to go into retreat at Chy Tralee and beg me not to put my hands in any way to anybody else's body, to bandage them up, not even to play the piano or feel the banister rail as I came downstairs, and that this would give me an excuse. But Sophie had failed me too. I played the piano. At any rate I would not talk to Amity this morning. I played without stopping. I thought that if I stopped Mrs. Nance might come and tell me that Amity was tired of reading and evidently wanted me to talk to her. I thought that Sophie might come and demand an explanation, though what she might need an explanation of I could not have said. I played the piano till the notes seemed to lose all resonance and sounded back on my ears with the dead, wooden sound of a xylophone that has been stored in a damp room.

The weather was coming right again. The sun was fitful yet, every now and then sunk in cloud, but it was persistent, and soon it would come out riotously hot. I would have preferred it cold.

In fact there was only one way of spending that day without wretchedness, and it was a way not possible three hundred miles from London. In London I should have spent the morning in bed, slowly risen, bathed and drunk tea at midday. By four o'clock I should have been dressed and have gone off to put myself in the hands of an experienced barber. He would have cut my hair, shampooed me with lovely, rubber vibration to enervate and then make tingle the scalp. He would have shaved me, steamed my face with hot towels and powdered me. I should then have gone out and lingered for three hours over a very good meal with the wines appropriate to every dish, after which I should have betaken myself to a Turkish bath and slept there until seven o'clock the following morning when I should have been ready for life again. That would have been the only harmless way of spending the day, and away down here at Rose Gwavas it was totally out of my reach.

So I played the piano till lunch.

After lunch I felt more in order, but I wasn't. I went up to Sophie's room, and we played a game which a man can only play when he is in a particular condition. It is necessary for him to have had his nervous sensibilities dulled, but he must not himself have lost all appetite. The game is played fully clothed. It usually begins in an easy chair, on the sofa or on the edge of a bed. The man preferably smokes a cigarette and pretends to be not in the least interested, while the poor, wretched girl scarcely knows what to do, but thinks the game might be fun once in a while and will take an occasional puff at the man's cigarette to show that she enters into the spirit of the thing. When the cigarette is burnt out, the game becomes steadily more strenuous. At last, after the two people have wrestled with each other through a great variety of uncomfortable positions which it would be painful to describe, the game usually ends up on the carpet by the door, the two people hot, exhausted and unhappy, and the man more likely than not only waiting for the moment at which he will not be thought impolite if he goes away to the bathroom to be sick.

9 June. Continuation of the same mood and . . . the adder.

I have the most vivid memory of stopping dead halfway upstairs and moving my hand up and down the banister rail to convince myself definitely that it was not sticky. I had been thinking of the house in which a young artist friend of mine at one time lived. When I visited him I never worried much about the smells, but the stickiness of the banister rail, where the children on other floors had left traces of jam, was a constant source of horror to me. It was associated for me with the last stages of every kind of squalor and humiliation, not to mention silver-fish in the lavatory.

'From the sense of touch, 'I thought, 'there is no escape. If an ordinary man lives in ugly, noisy or stinking places he can shut his eyes, plug his ears and put eau-de-Cologne upon his handkerchief, but there is no escape for the sense of touch. In addition to which, to finger anything, especially a living thing, affects the object. There is truly such a thing as the innocent eye. There is no innocent touch.'

In the afternoon I lay out on the great altar of granite behind the house, with the new sun burning down upon me. I dreamed of cords binding me down to the rock and awoke to feel a light touch on my arm. I thought it was Sophie and pretended to be still asleep. When at last I was called in to tea by Sophie she found at least half a dozen adders coiled up basking on the granite around me and when I asked her assured me that she had not been near me all the afternoon.

Mrs. Nance told me that I ought to be careful. A little girl down at Four Tides had died of an adder's bite only last year, and dogs were continually being stung.

John was not interested.

The next entry would, I feel certain, be allowed by the censor both in England and in the United States. My own private censorship does not allow it. If I try to concentrate on this particular day I find that my mind insists quite firmly on changing the subject or tells me that I ought to get up and go out for a walk or that I have a patient to visit in half an hour or that it would be very nice to play the piano.

It would be the entry marked 14 June, and if this story had remained under my control that would have been the most important date in it. As it is, the following day was more important because it was the day on which I partly caught up, on which I awoke to a little of the reality of what had been taking place in my absence.

15 June. Mrs. Nance's headache or, more significantly, the eve of Mrs. Nance's departure for London.

I think the headache was genuine, although I could not locate it.

'Wait a minute,' said I. 'I think I have some analine.'

And off I went for analine, orange-sticks and cotton-wool.

It was one of those headaches, was it? I felt worried. Mrs. Nance was having a bad time over something to get the sinuses all clotted up like that. I had already felt a vague ascription of guilt to me in her silence at supper and her request for my services immediately after.

I went back. Mrs. Nance was lying on the divan. packed up the cushions behind her neck to give an agreeable pressure in the right places.

'Thank you, Louis.'

She was giving me a look of gratitude, I knew, and her voice told me that I was a fundamentally nice, friendly man after all.

I soaked my two little wads of cotton wool, impaled them on the orange-sticks and inserted them slowly up Mrs. Nance's nostrils one after the other, away up farther than any vapour could reach. I had to feel the sensation of their going up in order not to irritate any delicate tissue on the way, and it gave me the beginnings of a sympathetic headache to do so.

'The main thing to do with that sort of head cold,' I said, 'is not to blow your nose. You couldn't inhale a vapour as high up as that, let alone blow the chambers clear. The fluid's a protection anyway, and the harder you blow the more inflamed all the empty passages become, and the tighter you close up inside, and the more your head aches.'

'Yes, Louis dear.'

'Now lie back and relax.'

Mrs. Nance laid her fine, leonine head back on the cushions, an orange-stick projecting from each nostril for all the world like the nose-ornaments of some barbarous,

African warrior. The fluid began to flow from the sinus chambers in her head, and I allowed her to keep dabbing her top lip with a handkerchief.

'Honest to God, I do look a fool, Louis.'

And immediately after she sighed.

I don't know just how conscious of their own subtleties women are on such occasions, but I felt that Mrs. Nance had chosen to look a fool and to be completely helpless in my hands in order that she might speak her piece without seeming to be jumping up and down on me emotionally. It was a specimen of her infinite tact.

She said:

'Louis, I'm going up to town in the morning, and I'm going to stay up until it's all over. I can't stand what's going on in this house.'

I sat beside her and listened to the faint noises of the heath outside and tried not to feel and above all not to behave like a shamed schoolboy.

Mrs. Nance went on.

'I expect you've been down a lot of tunnels,' she said. 'Tell me, Louis. Have you ever failed to come out at the right end?'

'Not lately,' I said.

Mrs. Nance sighed with relief.

'No. Well, I expect you'll muddle out this time as well. Only, Louis . . .'

Her sigh was almost a groan.

'. . . Only you aren't half kicking up a stew on the way, Louis. And I don't want any of my babies hurt.'

Pause.

'I'm an interfering old bitch, Louis. But honestly . . .'

She grabbed hold of my hand, and she was more deeply moved than I had known her.

'Louis,' she said, 'you are forgiving me, aren't you? But honestly you do muck about lately. You seem to be going about—well, I almost said blind, Louis—these last few days. You're not coming all over Nietzschean, are you? I mean, reading *Also Sprach*. . . . You're not cultivating the rights of the superior man, are you, and taking just what you want wherever you can find it? Be serious, Louis. . . .'

I had thought I was being serious.

'I mean to say, have you watched my John, for instance? There's a lot been happening to him, Louis.'

I had nothing to do but feel ashamed. I had not given John a thought for some time.

'And what about Sophie's ankle, Louis? We all know why people sprain their ankles at a crisis. But what are you going to do about it? You can't just leave it at taunting her for behaving according to the rules.'

Another pause. My ears began to drum.

'And what about Amity? For God's sake, Louis, what about Amity?'

Mrs. Nance had my hand tightly held in both hers. She made as if to shake me for reassurance, and one of the orange-sticks shot out of her nose. Luckily it had brought the cotton wool down with it.

I didn't propose to get excited.

'I've got a kind of locum,' I said. 'I'll give you his address before you go.'

I must not be panicked out of letting things happen in their own way. But I was in misery not to be able to make some really adequate response to Mrs. Nance just then.

I stopped outside Sophie's door, but did not go in. I thought she would have called me in if her ankle had been paining her sufficiently to want attention. I went on.

Yesterday afternoon Amity and I had stood together on the north jetty at Pentreath, and she had felt the vibration of the drifters' engines pulsing through the granite, and I had listened to the voices of men at work, both the Cornish voices of those busy with their little boats here and the colder, harder East Anglian voices of those unloading the big drifters at the outer end of the jetty. We had stood hand in hand like a pair of children, and Amity's fingers speaking into my palm had been full of wonder and the simplicity of a child's excitement on finding itself at home in a new, strenuous world in which it has as yet no part.

Coming back to Rose Gwavas I had been told that Sophie had fallen awkwardly while going upstairs. The atmosphere of the house had been tense. John had gone out and stayed out all night.

And there was another, more difficult memory, already distorted into the semblance of a dream.

I lay perfectly still. The walls of the cave were silted up with loose soil, and there was vegetation of some kind, I suppose a kind of moss. I lay motionless, waiting. Panic had died out of me, though I knew that if I were to move it would return. Outside in the woods lay terror, though what the terror was and what its source I did not know. I lay and waited for the sound of drums to begin, distantly at first and then coming steadily nearer. I waited calmly, for I knew that when the sound of drums had reached a dinning climax about my ears then the terror would soon be over. I turned and felt my hands. The palms of my hands were smeared with blood, and there was also a trickle of moisture in the rock. I wiped my hands on what I had taken to be moss. Access to the cave had been difficult.

Outside I knew the blonde, heavy girl was fumbling her way towards me. I did not dare to venture out into the air to meet her and call her in. With hands reaching out before her into the darkness she made her own way uncertainly towards me, and I must wait. For a moment fitful light as from the moon fell upon her tired breasts and the excessive, unmuscled smoothness of her belly and hips, and then it was totally dark again.

She must reach me and take shelter beside me before the first, delicate pulse of a drum, and yet to feel anxiety for her safe arrival would defeat all our hope.

Then of a sudden, without having perceived her arrival, I knew that she was beside me. And in that moment I heard the first, remote beat of a drum, as if it were no more than tapped with the drummer's little finger, a trial of the note before the music at last began to swell out and come towards me. I gathered together all my inner strength to meet the terror and what was more difficult than terror itself, the approach of indefensible joy.

CHAPTER ELEVEN

WHEN THE MIDSUMMER'S Eve party was first arranged I had taken it as a declaration of hostile independence on Sophie's part. In point of fact Sophie had not arranged it and acquiesced in it without enthusiasm, but my attitude to her at the moment was of such a second-rate quality that I had taken it for granted she had decided to go in quite noisily for pagan, Cornish whimsies because she knew I disliked them.

Mrs. Nance had duly gone off to London and left me with the feeling of being forsaken, a feeling that everybody had started grotesquely slipping away from me with the malignant intention of leaving me alone in a house full of my enemies.

For a few days the house had, in fact, been full of Betty des Voeux, Jill and Trevor Beed. They had been making a great deal of noise, going off on loud excursions and coming in to noisy, Bohemian meals, and then John's voice had ceased to be heard among them, and presently Betty des Voeux had started becoming more metallic than ever until, at the point where her voice had seemed as if it would reach a pitch too high to be audible to the human ear, she had disappeared too and only returned once or twice since with the apparent intention of removing Trevor Beed from his Jill's sphere of influence. At last that had stopped, too, and I heard nothing but the daily arrival of Jill and Trevor Beed, their attempts on Sophie's attention, their chatter about Midsummer's Eve and their eventual departure with kindly, puzzled comments on poor, old Soph. and how shirty she'd turned, poor gal . . . who had seemed to be trying very hard but without success to feel that Jilly and Trevor were important, adequate people.

'The behaviour of mice when the cat's away,' said I.

Sophie was crouching in front of the radiator, with a slip of silk in her hands. I fancied she had been airing it to put on and had then liked the dry heat on her skin and remained thus to think her thoughts, for when I came into her room the slip had begun to scorch, and there had been a steaming, clean smell that reminded me of wash-day at home when I was a child. Sophie's skin was hot, too, where the heat from the radiator reached it. I could feel down her sides a distinct line where the dry, electric heat came to, and all the rest was cool. It gave me a distinct memory of photographs displayed in an exhibition, for where the heat clothed her there also was bright light, and the rest was sunk deeply in shadow, a dramatically lighted nude.

I was half-minded to go away again without a word, for I did not quite know why I had come here in the first place, and now that I was here Sophie made no response whatever to my presence, neither rounding on me with recriminations nor welcoming me. My first impulse had been at all costs to break down her detachment, and I had made to caress her. I had put my mouth to the nape of her neck and my hands there to her sides. But her detachment was perfect. She had made no response whatever, not so much as a shrug of impatience or any sign or distaste for my touch or any tremor of inward excitement. Her skin had not begun to tingle under my fingers. Where it did not remain cold, the dry heat from the radiator had clothed it with impenetrable difference.

The only thing I could think of was:

'I thought you might want me to explain. . . .'

Sophie took that for the nonsense it was and did not trouble to reply.

I tried again.

'You're not going off with the others,' I said, 'leaping over bonfires?'

'Yes, in a moment. I was just changing.'

That led nowhere either.

I said:

'What are you going to do?'

'Do?'

'Now that . . .?'

'You're the male in question, not I.'

Yes, I knew. It was as simple as that. I could not evade responsibility by asking other people to take the initiative and allow me simply to respond.

'You still . . .'

'Don't be a fool, Louis.'

I knew. It was not for me to ask questions. I had better go away and not come looking for my decision in other people. And yet I felt there was something that could be said.

On the way out I tried again. Sophie had to go over the heath and out on the Land's End road to the highest point of the Chy Tralee land by Kingdom Come. I thought that I would go part of the way with her and then come back to Amity.

'Listen,' I said. 'It's a matter of precisely what you're thinking, of the male being active and the female . . well, speaking the responses. *He for God only, she for God through him . . .*'

'What on earth . . .?'

'With Amity I have the full sensation of male responsibility for the first time in my life.'

'Do you?'

Did I?

'She can neither see nor hear. I can lead her. You have eyes and therefore could not help leading me. You are more at home, more active in the world than I.'

'It isn't true.'

'It is true. You can't escape the pattern. The sun is only male to the moon's female because the sun has its own light. In respect of a blind person the one with eyes must always play a male part.'

Sophie did not reply at once. Her breathing became difficult, and her thoughts, I knew, were all tangled up. Then:

'In fact you think I want to mother you. Believe me, Louis . . .'

'I'm not saying that you want to. I'm saying that you would have to.'

'Louis, stop talking nonsense.'

I thought she would cry, but she controlled herself.

208

'John's in love with Amity,' she said. 'He's like you. She gives him the sensation of male responsibility for the first time in his life. But he's also in love with her. Are you?'

I did not answer. It was not a question that I knew the answer to.

'Are you, Louis? Louis, there is some kind of reality in . . . that, isn't there?'

'I suppose so.'

'But is there? Is there?'

Again I did not answer, and that was the end of trying to talk. Sophie wanted an answer now, and I would not produce one I do not think I have ever failed so badly in my life as I did on that Midsummer's Eve. Sophie's response was perfect. I see that now.

I stopped dead.

'Perhaps I should go back now.'

'Good.'

And Sophie walked straight on without attempting to point me the way back.

She spoiled the effect a little by turning and calling back to me:

'John wanted me to get rid of you, while he took Amity to the fire.'

Then she started running. And if I had not been full of myself I should have known that she would break down and cry as soon as she was out of hearing. But I was full of myself, and I was full now of impotent, destructive rage. For I had walked beside Sophie without keeping any account of the way we came, and now I had no sense of my direction back to the house. I turned and hoped that my feet would show me the path. A few yards, and I had plunged into the middle of bracken and caught at a bramble with my hand to save myself from falling. I stood where I was, trying to collect myself and trembling with a rage that seemed to have no outlet.

I got back to the path and stood quite still, controlling myself and preparing myself for the unwelcome job of walking very, very slowly, feeling my way back to the house if I could, but at any rate not losing the path. My anger burned down to a cold, methyl flame, steadied by the need of the moment, but still fed by the sense of humiliation, ready to flare up again as soon as I was no longer helpless.

It was at that moment that a stone came flying dangerously close by my head and landed in the bracken to the other side of me. I listened carefully in the direction from which the stone had come and heard a stirring of the bracken and then silence, a momentary stirring again and then again silence.

I thought:

'Mr. Nicky Polgigga.'

And I wanted to laugh.

I called out:

'Hello. . . .'

I would have liked to meet the lad here and perhaps empty out my anger on him by making him feel a complete fool. But there was no response. A moment later the bracken started rustling again, and whoever had thrown the stone at me was going away discouraged.

A moment later, and I heard the fainter rustle of

somebody coming towards me along the path.

It was Betty des Voeux.

She was feeling savage, too, with a kind of melo-dramatic, ridiculous savagery.

'Hello,' she said. 'Are you coming along to help us rid the country-side of witches?'

'I like witches,' I said.

'I don't.'

Then she laughed.

'I've seen you before,' she said.

And she was standing very close to me.

I thought:

'This would do very well as a cure for some kinds of bad feeling. It would be the totally unforgivable thing, and that is always helpful in putting an end to trouble-some thoughts.'

Betty des Voeux was, in fact, an extremely attractive young woman. And yet I could not help feeling her essential futility, her inevitable despair. And to feel that made me need to treat her as a person and feel pro-foundly sorry for her and not want to make use of her.

'It wouldn't help, would it?'

'Nothing would,' she said. 'But I suppose you're right. I'm going after Trevor, I think.'

We stood close together for a moment. I felt that in some way Betty des Voeux had sagged since I was last near her.

'A strictly functional woman,' I thought. 'She has no pleasure in living for its own sake, no simple, private voluptuousness. She enjoys playing tennis and no doubt plays both well and gracefully, because the game has, at any rate, an immediate, social purpose, but she can derive no pleasure from her own movements when she is alone. When she marries she will stop playing tennis, and all her movements will become clumsy and unwilling. She will put on weight. A real man could make her live, but it is not in the nature of her world that she should find or be found by a real man.'

But I had to get back to Rose Gwavas.

I said:

'Will you walk a bit of the way back to the house with me?'

She did, and in the drive I kissed her once for pure humanity's sake and as if to make her feel that she was indeed desirable.

'Wait a minute, though.'

I went into the house and called the servant girl and found that Amity had, in fact, gone out in the car with John. That settled it. I went back to Betty des Voeux.

'Will you come in?'

Betty des Voeux came in. I got her a drink.

The car pulled up dead with a great screech, and as its engine stopped we heard a great, wild peal of laughter, such laughter as I could not have imagined in the most awful of nightmares. It was the laughter of a single person possessed by the spirits of ten thousand decrepit, cackling hags and yet with the vibrant strength of a young animal present in it.

Amity was drunk.

We got to the front door as Jill and Trevor were helping Amity in, she still laughing madly, they talking excitedly and helplessly, twittering with fright about what on earth ought to be done. Sophie followed them in. She seemed to be more or less in her senses.

I took Amity by the hands and began to lead her upstairs, without a word to the others.

Her fingers were telling me things in a hot, excited way.

'John burned himself,' she said.

And out of her mouth came the awful, wild laughter again.

I led Amity to her room and made her lie down on the bed. I took off her shoes and stockings and her dress, and all the time her fingers kept groping into my hand, telling me things.

'The snakes all collect in a heap on Midsummer's Eve,' she said. 'They all roll up like a ball of string and coil themselves round and spit into the air, and the spittle's snake-stone, and a man has to catch it and ride away to the river before the snakes catch him. Snake-stones are glass things with streaks of red and white in them. They sell them at five a penny in the shops, and they're called glass alleys.'

Again the laughter, toneless and deafening.

'John burned himself. They were rolling a flaming cart-wheel down a hill and burning a tatter-man. John ran down the hill with the cart-wheel and burned himself. That's why we went away from the others. He wanted to find a chemist in the town. I drank sweet wine in a herbalist's shop. He keeps open as late as he likes, and it's very strong, John says.'

But she was quietening down. And as I was getting

her into a nightdress I heard the car start up again below in the drive.

Trevor Beed ran out of the house and was calling out:

'John. John, old boy. Where are you going? Come back, old boy.'

But John drove away from the house, and soon after I heard his car racing distantly along the road.

Presently Sophie sent Jill and Trevor Beed away. Betty des Voeoux, I suppose, had slipped away on her own.

Amity's excitement began to take a new form.

She kept pulling at me, putting her arms round my neck and pulling herself up to me, feeling at my face with her mouth, as I tried to get her into bed and cover her up.

The laughter had died down to a silly, incessant chuckle in her throat.

I had to begin to quieten her the way she wanted, until she lost interest. Then she wanted me to go away and get her a cup of tea. When I had made tea and brought it up from the kitchen she was asleep. As I went downstairs again she had begun to call out what sounded approximately like my name, with the same, incessant chuckle rattling drowsily in her throat. I thought I was going crazy too.

As I passed Sophie's door Sophie came out on the landing.

She said:

'Can I help, Louis?'

And when I had gone to my own room at last and got into bed she came in and lay beside me. I was trembling and tense. Sophie knew it and out of pure humanity simply wanted to be present so that I might presently relax a little.

When I did relax she got up and said:

Good night, you bloody fool.'

And then she went away to her own room.

CHAPTER TWELVE

JOHN DID NOT come near the house again that night or the following day. In the morning, too, we found that the one girl who lived in the house had gone away, and just before lunch a small boy came round with a note from the girl's mother to say that she did not propose to let her daughter enter that house again with such goings on, nothing but a lot of rogues and whores, and please to send her Mrs. Nance's address in London so that she could write for her daughter's wages and tell Mrs. Nance just what she thought about what went on in her house as soon as her back was turned. One of the local farmers also came round that day wanting to see Mr. John about damage caused to one of his out-houses by a blazing cartwheel, as well as a cow that had run away and broken a fence with fright and another that had its milk turned sour with all the sorcery that went on. Otherwise the day was spent with Sophie and myself continually in and out of the kitchen, drifting in and out like shadows, preparing tea and bits of bread and cheese, getting in each other's way at every conceivable juncture and saying not a word, either of us. Amity slept all morning and in the afternoon seemed perfectly well, but a little puzzled and fretful, obviously wanting nothing better than to be left alone.

I thought:

'The moment John comes back I will go away. I will get a call through to Mrs. Nance in London, to find out if she wants me to do anything in particular with regard to Amity, and then I will go. It seems that I have a peculiar gift for making other people behave in an extraordinary manner, rooting out their little weaknesses. When I have removed myself completely out of their orbit it may be they will all settle down again into the old routine. Or a new one. . . .'

But the thought gave me a terrible pang when I remembered that among these people I had included Sophie Madron.

I added as an afterthought:

'My own mistake was to look for a decisive experience in Amity Nance, when all I had done was to fall for a moment in love with the image of my own blindness. Amity will not be hurt. All this will be a dream to her, and she will retain it as a dream until some fatherly, middle-aged gentleman marries her. Then she will forget it. But it is not so easy for Sophie. She will suffer after I have gone.'

And still the pang continued, an emptiness below the heart to demonstrate that my thought was still inadequate.

'Very well, then,' I said. 'It is only right and appropriate that I also should suffer. I shall discover as soon as I am away from it all that I was truly in love with Sophie Madron, and the pain of having destroyed what I had will last for a long time.'

Fool that I was.

The morning after that I awoke early and went down into the kitchen to make tea considerably before seven o'clock. I had filled the kettle and put it on before I heard a deep sigh and realised that somebody else was there, sitting at the kitchen table. John, evidently. And I said nothing.

It was a very beautiful morning, already hot, with the dewiness, fresh earth and sun filling the kitchen itself with a morning delight.

From the way John kept holding his breath I fancied that he was trying to say something and probably something very angry and incisive.

I waited.

John's breathing eased off, and he said very calmly:

'You can't have Amity.'

I smiled.

John misread my smile and started breathing hard through his nose.

He said:

'Go on. Say it.'

And with his agitation the chair he was sitting on scraped on the kitchen floor.

I said:

'I've got nothing to go on about. Nothing at all. . . .'

And added gratuitously:

'. . . I'm going away this morning.'

John was silent. I made my tea, sat down at the table and took two or three sips. I was going to say something, offer him a chance, as it were, to make any demands on me that he might want to, and I found that John was crying, half-heartedly at first and then really going it, sobbing his heart out.

I could not help getting up, going over to him and putting my arms about his shoulders, though I expected that he would shrug me away. He didn't.

'I'm going to marry Amity,' he said.

And he said it as if it were a suggestion that had come from me and that he was now accepting. In a sense I suppose that was the case. But for me, Amity would have seemed to John inaccessible. He would have fallen in love with her stupidly and let her go. I had acted, in effect, as a sort of go-between.

The cloud began to lift off my own heart.

I sat in a first-class compartment and listened to the wheels of the train going round. Hot and raw their iron must be after a hundred miles. I felt like that myself on a train journey. It was a long, troubled sleep from which to awake more exhausted than before. At twelve o'clock I went along the corridor for the first lunch, and since this daily express was by no means busy to-day I stayed on through the second lunch and on again till three o'clock, drinking a very pleasant 1929 Burgundy that was just on the point of beginning to sour. Every now and then I took the glass off the ordinary watch that I only use to carry around with me on a journey and felt at the time. At four o'clock I had some tea brought to my compartment and derived a melancholy satisfaction from spilling it all over the awful, first-class plush. It is only on a train journey that I really dislike my fellow human beings, and even so I rarely feel quite unsociable enough to ride first class. I began to wish that I were travelling third now, if only to feed my wretchedness on other people's stupidities, with the qualification that it would have been no pleasure to spill tea on third-class plush.

During the last two hours of the journey I began slowly to come to life again.

I remembered John seeing me off, only John. We had said good-bye to each other in the tones of men swearing perpetual blood-brotherhood.

And I remembered taking my leave of Sophie in her room, where she had remained to rest because her ankle had started swelling again with unwise exertion.

The fool and his folly are not soon parted.

Even now I had left the last possibility to Sophie.

I had gone up and said:

'I've spoilt a lot of things, haven't I?'

And she:

'Yes, it's all a little messy now.'

'I'm sorry.'

'Me too.'

'Well. . . .'

And there I had left it.

I had wanted Sophie to say:

'But how much does it matter?'

I had expected her to say it. I had wanted her to make everything look all right in retrospect, and I had expected her to.

She would have said, I thought:

"Things are messy, always. Everything is a little messy. Perfection's impossible, and all we can do is to let things run at least their natural course."

But she had not.

I had thought that perhaps she would tell me she wanted to be alone for a while and that she would follow me to London in a month, a week or a few days. But she had said nothing of the kind, and I had driven away with John, with a feeling of destiny being accomplished and the final reflection that to think, expect or hope that folly could be mended now had been childish.

Now I was approaching London, and as I slowly recovered from the deathly effects of travelling things began to settle themselves into proper focus.

There were so many things that I knew. How did I contrive to forget them at the moment when just that kind of knowledge was essential to me . . . and to more than me?

'In man's decision is woman's peace.'

An old formula, and now it began to ramify to the rhythm of the train wheels.

'In my action alone her comfort lies.'

Fool that I was, yet wise enough now to know it. I had wanted her to set matters right for me.

'The only thing able to resolve these matters for her is decisive action on your part.'

Of course, of course.

I should have said:

'Follow me to London at the beginning of next week.'

'Louis. . . .'

'Promise.'

'Louis, I can't.'

'Promise.'

And I should have forced her to it or never consented to leave her for a second.

A curious exaltation took possession of me, though it was coupled with an equally curious anguish, anxiety to compel the whole thing to be adjusted instantly, the certainly of despair if I permitted myself to be excited for a single moment by hope. Hope was fatal, yes. Decisive action unfortified by hope was the only thing that contained in itself enough strength to move Heaven and earth, let alone a woman.

Now I must write to her. I must write quite definitely, in a way that permitted no evasion. And the possibility of a refusal I must consider not as something to be feared but simply as a technical possibility to be subsequently dealt with. Sooner or later I would fetch her.

If only the train would ride into Paddington Station quickly enough. And if only with the help of God and a taxi I could reach my desk before the fingers of my right hand lost their perfect resolution.

But the fool and his folly truly are not soon parted.

For a week I put off writing in order to be sure in my own mind that at any rate I did not merit a refusal or rather that I did merit the response that I wanted.

Mrs. Nance was out of London, visiting friends somewhere in the home counties. When she came back and stayed in London for a fortnight I was timid enough to wait for news of Sophie from her and to postpone writing to Sophie still further until I had it.

When at last Mrs. Nance did mention Sophie it was to say:

'Oh, by the way, Louis, Sophie's in town. You ought to go and see her.'

Sophie had, in fact, been in London for nearly a week. And she had not even let me know. I pointed out this fact to Mrs. Nance.

'So what, Louis Dunkel?'

Yes, so what?

I said:

'Have you got her address, then?'

'Of course I've got her address.'

And presently off I went, with the feeling that after all things that happened in London were quite as inexplicable as those that happened in the Duchy of Cornwall.

Sophie was staying with a girl who had a studio in Hammersmith. When I got there the other girl was out, and Sophie was drinking tea with a soft-voiced young man whom she appeared to know quite well. For a moment it depressed me to find that she had, at any rate, the elements of a life of her own in London, too, though I told myself the moment after not so be so damned possessive.

When the young man had gone I said:

'You didn't let me know you were here.'

Sophie spoke off-hand.

'No,' she said. 'I thought you'd find me out somehow or other if you wanted to.'

'Come and see where I live,' I said.

And Sophie came.

I said:

'What are you wearing now? I can't fit you into London yet. Are you very smart?'

'I have stockings on,' she said. 'And I have a costume and white gloves.'

'A red costume?'

'No, a black one. I've had it for years now. I alter it every year, and I wear it for a month or a week.'

The taxi was easing out of the main traffic now.

Sophie said:

'You live in Hampstead, then?'

'Yes, right on the heath.'

'How comic.'

'Why?'

'It just is. It would be comic if you lived in Baker Street or Wimbledon, too.'

'I hadn't looked at it like that, of course.'

'How do you get about in town, Louis?'

'I have the heath on one side of me and a cab-rank on the other, and I cater a great deal for people with cars. I'm a luxury trade, after all.'

We reached my door. I lived at the time in that great mass of jerry-built, brick houses which I am told look like a bulwark of the heath against the invasion of civilised Hampstead. I used to feel that it was true. The heath lay outside my back window, or at least Parliament Hill did, and I used to feel that people who lived even in other parts of Hampstead were outsiders whom we only allowed to pass through our midst on Sunday mornings and on bank holidays.

Sophie said:

'This is a solemn moment, Louis.'

224

I felt that she was a rather different person, more sophisticated here beside me in London. Or it may have been that she was excited. It may have been that she felt that a decisive step was at last being taken. Or it may have been my nervousness which distorted my image of of her, for nervous I was. And I suppose that I was nervous because a decisive step was at last being taken, in any case. Perhaps any step taken in a great city, a place which is entirely man's creation, is necessarily more decisive than the same step taken in the midst of a countryside where man is even now the least conspicuous inhabitant. Or perhaps it is simply more difficult in a great city to perform an act which really is an act at all and not a symbolic gesture, because it has to be performed in the midst of four million people who spend their lives performing symbolic gestures and scarcely ever perform an act which is really an act.

Sophie went into my back room.

'It's very nice,' she said.

The windows were wide open, and a breeze kept the curtains sweeping up and down across the window-sill and brought into the room a distant murmur of kite-fliers, promenaders and athletes on the heath.

I wanted to take Sophie in my arms, at once.

She said:

'Let me come in slowly and in a lady-like manner. I must take my gloves off. And my hat. I must tidy my hair.'

Oh, she was happy.

I said:

'Don't go away again now. I have a man in the cab-

225

rank who'll go to Hammersmith and collect your things.'

She didn't speak. I stood by the open windows. A second later I heard an odd, little sound in Sophie's throat which was half a swallow and half a little cough. Sophie was sitting on the divan now. I went and sat beside her and took her hands and presently put a hand to her face. The tears had formed in her eyes without beginning to fall, and she was sitting bolt upright, staring straight in front of her.

'I want to burst,' she said. 'And I mustn't, because I'm going out to supper with Auntie.'

Then she began to shake and weep in earnest and clung to me with her face on my shoulder, and I felt how piteously hot she was inside her clothes.

A matter of five minutes later she was going round the flat arranging one or two untidy things more to her liking and wanting to know where the nearest place was to buy flowers.

THE END

71
72
74
75
76
77
79
83
85